11/06

D0090833

# Nothing but the Truth (and a few white lies)

# Nothing but the Truth (and a few white lies)

Justina Chen Headley

LITTLE, BROWN AND COMPANY
New York · Boston · London

Little, Brown and Company

Time Warner Book Group
1271 Avenue of the Americas, New York, NY 10020
Visit our Web site at www.lb-teens.com

First Edition: April 2006

Library of Congress Cataloging-in-Publication Data

Headley, Justina Chen.
    Nothing but the truth, and a few white lies / by Justina Chen Headley.—1st ed.
        p.   cm.
    Summary: Fifteen-year-old Patty Ho, half Taiwanese and half white, feels she never fits in, but
when her overly-strict mother ships her off to math camp at Stanford, instead being miserable,
Patty starts to become comfortable with her true self.
    ISBN 0-316-01128-2 (hardcover)
    [1. Racially mixed people—Fiction.   2. Self-esteem—Fiction.   3. Mothers and daughters—
Fiction.   4. Prejudices—Fiction.   5. Single-parent families—Fiction.   6. Taiwanese
Americans—Fiction.   7. Stanford University—Fiction.]   I. Title.
PZ7.H3424Not   2006
[Fic]—dc22

                                                                    2005022021


10  9  8  7  6  5  4  3  2  1

Q-FF
Printed in the United States of America
The text was set in Berkeley Book, and the display type is Syntax.

For Tyler and Sofia,
my hapa kids who are wholly wonderful

Nothing but the Truth (and a few white lies)

# 1 ∘ Belly-Button Grandmother

While every other freshman is at the Spring Fling tonight, I have a date with an old lady whose thumb is feeling up my belly button.

I turn my head to the side and catch a whiff of mothballs and five-spice powder on Belly-button Grandmother's stained silk tunic and baggy black pants. At this moment, Janie and Laura are dancing in the gym that's been transformed into a tropical paradise for the last all-school dance of the year. Me, I'm stretched out on this plastic-covered sofa with my T-shirt pushed up to my nonexistent chest and my pants pulled down to my boy-straight hips.

"You gonna get in big accident," announces Belly-button Grandmother in her accented English, still choppy after living in Seattle for over fifty years. She smacks her lips tight together, which wrinkles her face even more, so that she looks like a preserved plum. The fortune-teller closes her eyes and her thumb presses deeper into my belly button.

"When you fifteen," she says. A bead of sweat forms on her forehead like she can feel my future pain.

I muffle a snort, *Yeah, right.* Considering my life is nothing but school, homework, and Mama, broken with intermittent insult-slinging with my brother, there's hardly any opportunity for me to get in a Big Accident.

"*Aiya!*" mutters Belly-button Grandmother, on the verge of another dire prediction.

If my mom wanted my future read, why couldn't she have found a tarot reader? I'm sure somewhere in the state of Washington there's a Mandarin-speaking, future-reading tarot lady. Or a palmist who'd gently run her finger across my hand. Someone who would say, *My goodness, what a long happy life you're going to have.*

But no, my future is being channeled through my belly button.

As soon as Mama heard from The Gossip Lady in our potluck group about Belly-button Grandmother, she packed me up and hauled us both down the freeway. This is my mom, the woman who drives only in a five-mile radius around our home, a whole hour south of Seattle. The woman who has driven on a highway maybe twenty times *ever.* The same woman who looks at maps the way I look at her Chinese newspapers: unreadable.

Belly-button Grandmother's bone-dry thumb presses harder into my stomach like she wants to dig right through me. If she presses harder, I won't have a future. I wince. She scowls. I would say something profound like, *Hey, that hurts!* if I wasn't afraid that the old lady was going to change my future.

Belly-button Grandmother sighs like my life is going to be filled with even more disaster than it is now with this Mount Fuji–sized pimple on my chin.

"You gonna have three children. Too many," she pronounces. For a brief moment, she releases the pressure on my belly and stares down at me with her cavern-dark eyes. "You want me take away one?"

I want to say, *Get real.* How can I even think about conceiving three kids, much less discuss family planning, when I can't even get a date to my school dance?

Belly-button Grandmother's frown deepens as if she read my insignificant thoughts. Her thumb hovers over my stomach. Quickly, I shake my head. I don't need my mom to translate the look on the fortune-teller's face: *Oh, you making a big mistake.*

Now I turn my face to the side so I don't have to look at Belly-button Grandmother and her disapproval anymore. Above the couch, white paint is peeling off the wall next to the picture of Buddha, his smooth, flat face serene. I wonder what other predictions he's heard Belly-button Grandmother make and whether he's having himself a good belly laugh about how the closest I've ever gotten to Nirvana is winning a sixth-grade essay contest about why I loved being an American. My field trip to Nirvana was a short one. Steve Kosanko didn't see me as anywhere close to being a true red-white-and-blue American. The day after I won the contest, he cornered me at recess and serenaded me with a round of "Chinese, Japanese, dirty knees, look at these." As an encore, he held me down in the mud like it was some squelchy rice paddy where my dirty knees belonged.

Another sniff, this time of incense, makes me want to gag. I need to sneeze, but rub my nose hard instead. A sneeze would probably contract my abs, and then, God, my whole life course could be altered.

What I really want to know, desperately need to know, is whether Mark Scranton, Mr. Hip and Cool at Lincoln High, will ever notice me. Well, technically, he does notice me. I did write his campaign speech, after all. But it's too much to hope that I'll actually get a chance to date him, not with Mama's no-dating-until-college edict (strike one), Mark being a white guy (strike two) and me being a bizarrely tall Freakinstein cobbled together from Asian and white DNA (strike three). I'm out before I've even scooted off the bench.

So a more realistic miracle that I'll take to go, please, is an Honors English essay, one that needs to be started and finished this weekend. The same essay that the rest of the class has worked on for nearly the entire year.

I don't need a miracle, tarot reader, palmist, or even a Belly-button Grandmother to tell me what my mom is doing out in the waiting room. She's praying to Buddha: "Please let my daughter marry a rich Taiwanese doctor." But then, in an act of practicality, she amends her prayer: "A Taiwanese businessman would be acceptable. Acceptable but not ideal."

I would've settled for an acceptable but not ideal date to my Spring Fling.

Belly-button Grandmother yanks her thumb out of my belly button and calls sharply, "Ho Mei-Li!"

The door opens immediately. Mama's face tightens as she peers accusingly at me. Her permed hair is a damp halo around her furrowed brow. She glances at me and speaks in a rapid Mandarin so that I can't follow what they're saying.

I tug my T-shirt down and sit up. Who needs a translator when I see my mother's frown and the shake of her head as Belly-button Grandmother chatters?

"*Be-gok lan?*" Mama says, slipping into Taiwanese in her shock.

Belly-button Grandmother nods once, solemnly, even though she doesn't understand Taiwanese. Whatever the language, I have no problems divining what's being predicted here. According to my navel, I am going to end up with a white guy.

Mama glares at me: *Oh, you making a big mistake.*

I walk to the window overlooking the International District, all crowds of black heads and neon lights. And I'm surprised that I just want to go home. Not out to my favorite Chinese restaurant, not even to the dance, but to my bedroom.

I touch my belly button. Maybe there is magic in there after all.

I know what I'd wish for.

As Mama and Belly-button Grandmother confer about my life, I rub my stomach three times for good luck, just as if I were a gold statue of a big-bellied Buddha.

Then I wish to be white.

## 2 ∘ Mama-ese

After we collect my big brother, Abe, who's been poring over Japanese comic books in a *manga* store, Mama conducts the Chinese Food Census, her preferred method for selecting a restaurant. No studying of menus or trusting food critics for Mama. Instead, she stares into a window — never mind if she freaks out some poor diner who happens to be eating by said window — and tallies the number of black-haired heads inside a restaurant.

Her theory is straightforward and accurate: a high black-hair-to-blond ratio equals a good Chinese restaurant. High blond-to-black-hair equals food fit for pigs. I would have said dogs, but some people are under the misconception that all Asian people eat man's best friend. We don't. The only part of a dog I have tasted — by accident when I laughed while within licking distance of a golden retriever — was its slobbery tongue. However, inquiring minds want to know why we don't hear people retching over the Rudolph-the-Red-Nosed-Reindeer-eating Norwegians or the whatever-the-hell-is-haggis-chewing Scottish.

Mama squints, shakes her head and scurries on, passing one restaurant after another. Finally, we're sitting inside a Cantonese restaurant, packed with huge families, loud chattering intergenerational micro-villages. Our tiny family of three is a raft bobbing in a sea of Chinese conversations. A lone wave of English washes over from a Tourist Family, who are goggling like they've flown into Shanghai, not Seattle. Over in the corner by the fish tank, a herd of kids pounds on the aquarium, but the fish don't swim away. I want to warn those cooped-up fish, *Beware of the Big Net*. Since fighting is futile, I don't say a word.

Above the Mandarin and Cantonese, the clicking of chopsticks, the pouring of tea, Mama and I face off. We sit across the table from each other like two generals negotiating a delicate truce. At the far side is Abe, Switzerland in this battle of words. His dark eyes are locked on the dumbed-down English menu like he's cramming for a final tomorrow in a class I could teach: Multiple Disorders of Dysfunctional Half-Asian Families.

"You going to summer camp," Mama announces to me without looking down at her menu.

My heart stops. I can already picture the hell that my mother wants to send me to. You can bet that this is no camp with horseback riding or archery. There'll be no in-depth sessions on anything remotely cool, say multidimensional printmaking or Italian cooking. My stomach starts making worrisome gurgling noises as I recall the "accelerated learning programs" Mama made me apply to for the summer.

All I know is that I better parry back, and fast. "No, I'm going to be working. Remember, you said I had to get a job this summer."

Score two points for me.

"You don't have job."

Five points for Mama. But I recover quickly: "I've got three weeks before summer starts. And Belly-button Grandmother said that I was going to find a great job."

Shoot, Mama frowns and leans toward me. "When you out of college. No job at mall again. You spent more than earned last summer."

Ouch. Ten points for Mama. From the grim look in her eyes, I can tell she's not finished with this volley. Like always, she goes from our current fight to future doom-and-gloom in two seconds flat. "You need save money. Work hard. Go to good college. Get good job. Take care of self. No one take care of you once I gone." Her lips purse the way they do whenever she makes an oblique reference to my long-gone father, still a sour memory after thirteen years.

I make a tactical error; I hesitate when I should push back hard with a comeback.

Like the brilliant fighter that she is, Mama drops the bomb just as a stocky waiter stops at our table: "You going to math camp."

"*Math* camp?"

"At Stanford." Mama becomes too engrossed in ordering our dinner to embellish further. Anyway, she's won this skirmish.

While Mama's conferring with our waiter about the freshness of the pea vines, I'm steaming like braised cod. A week with geeks while my friends are funning in the sun? I deliberately torpedoed my application to math camp by asking the one teacher I was sure hated me to write the mandatory recommendation. Obviously, my torpedo was a dud. Or was it? Mr. Powell couldn't be taking revenge on me for me talking one too many times in his Geometry class, could he? Considering that we were studying tangents, I thought my own about maximum heel height before you approach sluttiness was an appropriate application of the concept. (Incidentally, the consensus was three inches for the optimal sexy-to-slutty ratio.)

"*Bo po mo fo,*" mutters Abe, sneaking a peek over his menu. He's barely containing a laugh.

I choke on my jasmine tea. Suddenly I'm tripping down memory lane to the year when Mama read an article about China's enormous potential as a trade partner. Never mind that Abe was in third grade and I was in kindergarten. No matter, the two of us were going to learn Mandarin, our first baby step to financial security. While all the three-year-olds sailed through to the conversation classes, Abe *bo-po-mo-fo*'ed his way through the Chinese alphabet for an entire year. Mama finally realized she was just wasting her money on Abe, and he became a proud Chinese School Dropout. Unlike me, the Chinese School Drudge who had to keep going until junior high.

"What's Abe doing this summer?" I ask as soon as Mama finishes with the waiter. I figure, whatever Abe's doing, I'll do, too. After all, this is *my* survival, my summer, my reputation at stake.

Abe reluctantly hands over his shield of a menu to the waiter. Vulnerable to attack, but highly trained in survival tactics, Abe gives up neutrality. He cracks his knuckles the way he does before pitching a no-hit game, and blurts out, "I'm going to be so busy preparing for Harvard."

The Harvard card, I should have guessed he'd play it. Three hundred points for Abe.

Mama nods, looking at him proudly. Bonus, twenty points.

Since the thick crimson acceptance packet was wedged in our mailbox a couple of months ago, Abe has transformed from Boy Who Wasted His Time Weight Lifting to the Pride of the Potluck Party. For once, Abe is the kid all other Asian parents compare their children to. I mean, why else is Mama so thrilled to host the upcoming potluck party? Abe's given her a free pass for the next century to boast, brag, and generally rub his brilliance in the envious faces of her so-called friends.

"Like what?" I demand. "What do you have to 'prepare'?"

Abe shoots me a dirty look.

"I've got to pack my room, and I've got a job," Abe, the perfect eldest son, responds.

Presto-chango! Witness another magical transformation, care of Harvard. Suddenly, being a lifeguard trumps tutoring for big bucks like he did last summer.

"You meet some nice girls," says Mama to me, wiping her chopsticks on the paper napkin before arranging them straight on her plate. "And boys."

I have a reasonable handle on English, can speak Taiwanese as well as a preschooler and could find my way around in Spain. My grasp of Mandarin has faded to the first four letters of the alphabet, "thank you," "this is delicious," and "you are a bad daughter." But I am absolutely fluent in Mama-ese: a "nice" boy means he's Taiwanese.

Not Japanese.

Not Korean.

Not even *gua-shing lan* — those Nationalist Chinese who fled the mainland and overran Mama's beloved Taiwan some fifty years ago.

And certainly not white. Having two half-Asian kids obviously hasn't made up for the great regret in Ho Mei-Li's life: marrying that *yang gweilo*. Well, what do you know? Two more Chinese words I remember. How can I forget such an appropriate term to describe my father — the white foreigner ghost whose absence haunts our lives?

"Great, I get to date geeks," I mutter.

"Not date!" Mama shakes her head emphatically. "It take long time know someone. Find Good One first. Then be friends long time. Then marry."

Subtext: don't pick a Bad One the way Mama did.

I check my watch. At that second, the only Good One I want, Mark, is probably slow dancing with his date, the most beautiful, blond junior varsity cheerleader in Lincoln High history. That thought mummifies my heart, wrapping it in endless layers of wanting but not having.

I don't need to go to summer math camp to add one plus one. One: Mama must be so rattled by Belly-button Grandmother's prediction that I'm going to end up with a white guy that she's pushing me to fish for a nice Taiwanese boy. Plus one: said Taiwanese fishing hellhole is math camp at Stanford. Equals: I am so screwed.

Negative infinity points for me.

"Oh, dis-GUST-ing!"

For a split second, I think I've yelled out loud. But no, it's Teenage Tourist Girl leaping out of her chair. Glowering, the waiter holds a bucket before her table. A fishtail flops over the brim, and Mom Tourist joins in with a shriek. The waiter stalks off, his face tight because how would you like to be part of some strangers' anecdote for the next twenty-five years? *Look! They actually bring you a live fish! Can you imagine that?*

The same waiter hauls a bucket to our table, glaring like he's practically daring me to make a scene, too. But it's not *me* the waiter should be worried about. Mama nods *fine* to him and our netted fish, and turns her eyes back to me.

"I don't want to go," I say feebly, knowing it's futile to fight The Big Net that is my math summer camp.

Mama glowers at me. Oh, no, here we go again . . .

And she bites out the dreaded words: "You have it so easy."

## The Mama Lecture Series
## Lecture 1: You Have It So Easy

Greetings and welcome to The Mama Lecture Series, brought to you by the first-generation Mamas who left the Old Country for Brand-New America. But first, a message from our proud sponsors. While audience participation, such as talking back, is forbidden, tears of guilt and effusive apologies are more than welcome. Please be advised that there is no need for copious note-taking. These lectures are freely given at every possible opportunity. And we do mean, *Every. Possible. Opportunity.* Thank you so much and enjoy the show.

"You have it so easy," Mama repeats, jabbing her chopsticks in the air at me with each point she makes, not caring that her voice is escalating or that everyone in the restaurant is watching. "Whenever you want something, you hold your hand out. You need a new book? I give it to you." Jab. "You need some new pants. I give it to you." Poke on the table. "You need, you need. When I was little, we so poor even though my father was dentist. But who could pay him? Not with money." A couple of raps on her empty plate. "Maybe a little rice. Or a chicken. We were so poor sometimes my mother grind up *cockroaches* for us to eat."

At this point, I know better than to gasp in disbelief or contort my face into a disgusted expression. Audience interaction like this usually means an unwanted and often-prolonged jaunt into Ingrate Land.

Still, Mama sniffs indignantly, as if to say, *Can you believe how much I have suffered in my life?* Trust me, I can. I stare down at my hands clenched tightly on my lap. Honestly, what's unbelievable is that I'm not hunchbacked with guilt from the number of times she's told me and Abe how easy her life would have been if she had only married her Taiwanese suitor. Not our white guy of a dad. As if *we* chose our father, not she.

Mama breathes in sharply. She must be smelling my exasperation polluting the air.

"You think you too good to eat ground-up cockroach?" Mama scowls at me. "If you starving, you hold your hand out for cockroach. You say, please don't grind up. I eat whole."

I catch Teenage Tourist Girl looking like she's going to projectile vomit. She shrieks, "Gross!" while staring at me with her mouth misshapened with disgust like I am a Teenage Tourist Girl from some primitive civilization. For the first time since this miserable day started, I am glad that the all-school dance is tonight because it means that no one I know, especially Mark, can waltz in and witness just one more moment in the Patty Ho Hall of Mothering Shame.

Mama finally recalls the purpose of her lecture, which is not to reminisce unhappily about long-ago hard times so much as to give me a hard time for my in-her-face too cushy of a life. She shakes her head like it's a saltshaker full of self-pity: "I would have given everything to attend math camp if I had the opportunity."

The *coup de grace,* like always, gets delivered in a tone of deep disappointment: "You are so lucky."

When this lecture is delivered in the comfort of our own home, my shriveled-up shitake mushroom of a heart usually gets a good rehydration when I cry on my bed. One that I am so lucky not to have to share with a sister the way Mama did growing up.

Here in the restaurant, the bad part of me (OK, the ungrateful daughter in me) wants to say, "If I'm so lucky, then why did Daddy leave me here with you?"

But of course, I keep my mouth shut.

# 3 ○ The Truth About Banana Splits

Any mention of the "H" word — homework — usually stops all of Mama's lectures in their tracks. So as soon as I step through the front door, painted cherry red last summer to flag down some good luck to our house, I plaster a serene expression on my face. Instead of saying, *Thanks for another anti-pep talk, Mama* like I want to, I force my mouth to say, "I've got a report I have to write by Monday."

If my brain weren't whirring with worry, I'd give thanks, cry hallelujah, weep tears of gratitude for my ability to procrastinate. My laziness has saved me from hours of lecturing.

I can't run up the rosy carpeted stairs to my bedroom fast enough. I've had it with Mama and her quack of a fortune-teller and her warped idea of summer fun being equating while trolling for some "nice" Taiwanese boy. All I want is a nice soccer boy named Mark.

I jerk open my bedroom door even as every brain cell is screeching, *Don't do it!* What lies ahead of me is a blank computer screen. Suddenly, I wonder if I shouldn't suffer Mama's lecture. You know, I could just focus on her moving mouth and fill in other words like a badly dubbed foreign flick. Who am I kidding? There's no time to play the subtitles game with Mama tonight. I've got to write an entire fiction about myself.

What I haven't told Mama, what I've been trying to pretend all year that I've got under control, is that the essay is due Monday, thirty-six hours away, and I haven't had the guts to jot down a single word.

On the first day of the year, Mrs. Meyers announced to our Honors English class, "In three years, you'll be applying to colleges and your competition isn't the person sitting next to you."

You could have heard every one of our brain cells churning as we all thought, *It's not?* We stared at Mrs. Meyers, willing her to tell us who was. Tiny, dark, and handsome, she simply smiled her Sphinx smile at us as if she hadn't caused shock waves to course through the class. Rumor had it that Mrs. Meyers was too smart to be a high school teacher. Rumor also had it that her husband was some computer guru who had hit it rich in the Silicon Valley. Why someone would willingly subject herself to this hellhole, better known as High School, was beyond me. But there I was, watching her like a kid at a magic show, completely transfixed.

"The young people you will be competing with to get into Harvard, Stanford, Princeton, Yale, any of the top-tier universities," Mrs. Meyers said in her lilting, perfectly cadenced King's English, "aren't the students in Twin Harbor. They're the ones at the private schools in Seattle: University Prep, Seattle Academy, Bush. Lakeside had *triple* the admittance rate to those universities compared to Lincoln." She crossed her thin arms. *"Triple."*

Was it my imagination or did I just hear the morale in our class splinter into tiny slivers? Next to me, my best friend, Janie, shot me a can-you-believe-this-crap look as she silently bid her spot at Brown good-bye.

But Mrs. Meyers was just getting started. "You can bet that each of those students has been practicing writing essays since second grade. They know how to write beautifully crafted sentences and smart, articulate paragraphs. They will write compelling college essays, ones that will prove that they are intelligent. Accomplished. Would thrive in any Ivy League."

"So we shouldn't even bother to apply, is that it?" asked Anne Wong, a new transfer student from the Land of Bizarre. Both her parents are engineers, so maybe that explains her intensity. Or not.

"But," said Mrs. Meyers, holding one finger up, "the one thing those students haven't been taught is to write about . . ."

We waited as Mrs. Meyers, looking almost dreamy, now fixed her coffee-colored eyes out the windows. What was she thinking of while we were sweating it out? How far she had come from her hometown in India? Why she was wasting her time with a bunch of Waspy kids?

Finally, Anne blurted what we were all thinking: "What?"

Mrs. Meyers stepped to the clean chalkboard. Slowly, she picked up a piece of chalk and scrawled one word: *Truth.*

"What does *that* mean?" Anne muttered even as she copied it down into her notebook. I couldn't help cringing. Why did Anne have to be such a good, studious, brainy Asian student?

"It means that Cole's going to write about what a dork he is," called out Mark, his enormous brown eyes crinkling at the sides as he grinned. Looking altogether quite adorable, I might add. Jordan, his freckle-faced soccer buddy, cackled along with him.

"It means," said Mrs. Meyers, perching on the edge of her desk and swinging one leg like a young girl, "that this year, all of you are going to write the Truth about yourself. What matters to you. What you believe in."

Mark and Jordan stared at her, joking forgotten. For all of us, the realization sank in that the rumors about Mrs. Meyers were true. Not a single one of us was going to escape her scrutiny, which meant that we'd actually have to work in this class.

Mrs. Meyers stopped moving her leg and leaned ever so slightly toward us, her voice dropping to a low, conspiratorial tone. "Because you cannot begin to write any personal statement, answer any college essay, until you know who you are. And that is what freshman year is all about — self-discovery." She laughed lightly and ran one hand through her short, dark hair, a dime-sized diamond winking at us. "The Truth, and nothing but the Truth. And, by the way, half of your grade at the end of the year will be based on what you write."

So here I am in a bedroom that looks like Christmas gone Chinese with a green shag carpet and five sprigs of lucky bamboo jammed into a vase, oxblood red for fortune, of course. With three weeks left to go of freshman year, all I've got is my name in the center of an otherwise empty page on the screen.

I lean against my chair and look up for divine intervention.

There isn't so much as a single crack in the ceiling for me to draw some inspiration from. Nothing but smooth white surface, drywall covering up all the family secrets in our home, like *Where's my father? Why did he really leave us?*

Tapping my foot on the floor impatiently, I wonder how exactly I'm supposed to write the Truth when I don't even know those basic facts about my life. Besides, what's the point of writing a Truth Statement when half the time people embellish the Truth to make themselves feel better (*I am so a 34B, and don't let Abe convince you otherwise*).

I sigh. The sad truth is, my computer screen is still blank. And I still have no idea where to start.

Since my belly button was enough of a portal to divine my future, perhaps it would be a source of deep insight. I touch my belly button. But all I can think about is how Belly-button Grandmother's prediction is sending me to math camp. Math camp?!? Look, if I'm going to end up with a white guy anyhow, couldn't it pretty please be Mark? For a moment, I indulge in my favorite fantasy of him finally falling down at my feet, struck with the epiphany that I am the love of his life.

A toilet flushes downstairs, and with it goes my dream.

The reality is, Mark and his blond pom-pom are dancing their night away at the Spring Fling. Me? I'm sitting my night away with my computer for a date, and Mama's expectations and Belly-button Grandmother's predictions as chaperones.

There's nothing to do but write. So I close my eyes like I can't face that truth, and start to type.

# The Truth as I Know It
## By Patty Ho

Truth: I am Patricia Yi-Phen Ho. Patty to my friends; Patty-cake to the one aunt on my mother's side who calls us once a year, and Pattypus to my enemy, Steve Kosanko, a short, stocky bully who's hated me since fourth grade. He's right in a way. I may not look half-duck, half-beaver, but I don't look wholly anything either. Not quite white, not all yellow.

My last name practically begs for a bad joke and, trust me, I've heard them all. Yo Ho Ho: preschool circle time. Mrs. Mannion chuckled along with the rest of the kids and then pretended that she hadn't. Heigh Ho! Heigh Ho!: circa third grade, chanted to me on the way to gym before I Red-Rovered all over everyone and was put into a time-out. And of course, Ho, present day, as called out by Steve Kosanko, aforementioned racist pig, as in "Yo, whore." Given my dateless status, a bit ironic, no?

Truth: I am a fourteen-year-old stick-thin giant who is imprisoned in the house of midgets. My mother barely squeaks over five feet tall, and calling my big brother Abe "big" is a misnomer when I'm a good five inches taller than him. I have to assume that my height comes from my father, but he's a short story in our home. It goes something like this: Once upon a time, Stanley Peter Johnson transferred from Berkeley to study at the University of Taipei for a year. He conquered, he came, and he left with a couple of made-in-Taiwan souvenirs: my mom and Abe. Apparently, his American Dream didn't include a mixed-race family of four. So for my second birthday, he gave me a good-bye kiss and vanished. End of story.

Truth: I live in Twin Harbor, which was named "one of the most picturesque cities in America." There are only 1.53 percent Asians here. Is there a connection between those two facts, I want to know. In any case, my house may as well be up at the North Pole, blanketed in white, because there are nothing but white people as far as my eyes can see. (To be totally accurate, since I *am* an accountant's daughter, in my high school of five hundred kids, there are two African-Americans, four whole + two half Asians, one Latino, and one Native American. Tell me that I don't live in perpetual whiteout.)

Truth: I believe in the 80/20 rule. Two of the cross-country team qualified for Regionals; the rest of us eight were their private pit crew–slash–cheering squad. Six of the biology class understood DNA; the rest of us were tangled in a double helix of confusion. Abe got eighty percent of the Mama-looking genes in our family; I got the dregs. There is no mistaking whose son Abe is with his jet-black hair, high cheekbones, and flat rice cake of a butt. Take a look at any Ho family picture and guess which one doesn't look like the others? Hint: the gawky girl with brownish hair and large eyes with a natural eye fold that Korean girls have surgically created. It's as if God cruised through one of those Chinese fast-food buffets and bought Abe the full meal deal so he can pass for Mama's beloved son. When it came to my turn, all that was left was one of those soggy egg rolls that doesn't qualify as real Chinese food.

But it is also true that I can pass. I can pass biology (miraculously), notes in class (well), and plates of food (perfectly). I cannot pass out (Why be out of control when I'm never in control in my prison cell of a home?) or pass a basketball (which bombs the theory that all tall kids can be basketball stars).

But I cannot pass for white or Asian.

So I am not a banana, yellow on the outside and white on the inside. And I'm not an egg, a white kid who gets off on all things Asian. I suppose that makes me a banana split or scrambled eggs. Too bad they both make me gag.

The final, absolute truth is this: I have visited an old woman to predict my future. I know as certainly as I know my zodiac signs, both Western (Cancer) and Eastern (tiger), that Belly-button Grandmother's predictions will change my life.

Not her prediction about my having three kids. To that, Mama said, "Don't worry. I help you," already picturing herself as a proud *Amah* even though Belly-button Grandmother had offered a free psychic family reduction session within thirty days of our visit.

Not the one that I would be a successful businesswoman when I grow up, which, frankly, takes a load off my mind since I haven't been able to find a summer job.

Not even her prediction that I'd get into a huge accident when I am fifteen, which gives me six weeks of health left in my life.

What will change my lame life as I know it is Belly-button Grandmother's conviction that I will end up with a white guy.

And that is the truth.

# 4 ∘ Tonic Soup

The morning after Mama hijacked me to visit Belly-button Grandmother, I wake up to a stench. Burnt leather with a touch of white pepper. I hide my head under my pillow and hope that this isn't another one of Mama's misguided attempts to cook meatloaf or hamburgers. Sometimes it's better for the world at large if we stick to what we do best, me with my English classes and Mama with her Chinese cooking.

By the way Mama's banging around the kitchen, it's obviously time to get up. Pots clatter and clash; Mama's Wok-and-Roll Band. I swing my legs off my bed and slouch on the edge, trying to gather up the energy to move, but I'm tired from my late night True Confession to my computer.

When I glance over to my desk, what little energy I have leaches out of me, drop by drop, and I've been awake for all of two minutes. I'm no neat freak: my clothes are crammed in my closet in no particular order; my bathroom drawers are cluttered with makeup I'm not supposed to wear. But I can't breathe if my desk is a mess. Strange, I know. But books belong in the bookshelf over in the corner, not stacked up on the ground. Pencils sharpened to needle points should line one drawer, instead of lying like stumpy logs carried downstream by a trickle of ideas. My college-ruled and graph paper should fill up my bottom shelf, not carpet my floor.

I try not to breathe too deeply because the stink is stronger than ever. Whatever Mama is brewing cannot possibly be edible. I walk on top of my discarded thoughts, feeling the paper crumple under my bony, bare feet. To tell the truth, I'm tempted to leave my used-up paper where it is because it looks a heck of a lot better as flooring than my lime green shag carpet. When carpet texture becomes hip twice in a lifetime, that usually means it's time to be replaced. But the likelihood of that happening in a house where napkins get ripped in half so that a package can go farther is close to nil.

See, I can do math.

Minus the math camp.

Irritated because I just remembered my summer that I was trying so hard to forget, I grab my pencils and stab them one by one into the electric sharpener. Just as I bend down for an armful of books, my bedroom door flings open and knocks the stack right onto my foot.

"Ouch!"

Obviously, concern for other human beings isn't a requirement for Harvard. Abe, his usually combed hair now suffering from a serious case of bed-head, just sniffs the air and groans, "God, what *is* that?"

"Rise and barf!" I manage to say in a chipper voice, even as my foot throbs. I rub it hard to dull the pain. "Mama's new way to wake us up in the morning."

My humor is lost on Abe. He looks pale. He's also not tossing a ball between his hands — baseball, basketball, tennis ball, you name it — which means that Boy Wonder is *really* feeling bad. So Mr. Harvard went partying behind Mama's back again, I think to myself.

If I had parties to go to, I'd hit Abe up for his tricks on sneaking out of the house. So far, that's one mystery I'm not destined to solve in this life.

Downstairs in our tiny kitchen, Mama acts like the reek of whatever's bubbling in the pot doesn't bother her nose. But since her super-smeller can sniff out the smallest smidgen of white pepper in chicken broth, I know she's faking it. Even through my pinched nose, there's no escaping this pungent odor.

Abe stumbles to the back door, fanning it open and closed in a hopeless attempt to clear the air. His eyes are shut, nose wrinkled. I wonder if he's going to throw up, because he's looking about as green as my bedroom carpet.

"This is for *Mei-Mei*," announces Mama, ladling a murky brown liquid into a large bowl.

"*I'm* not eating that," I tell her.

"Belly-button Grandmother say you need Tonic Soup."

Tonic Soup? Try Toxic Soup. The smell was bad enough, but its name just confirmed what I had been fearing: Mama whipped up some strange new Chinese concoction.

"What's Tonic Soup?" I demand, starting to back out of the room. "Why do *I* need to eat it?"

Mama's eyes glue me to my place on the linoleum floor, cutting off my retreat. Her lips tighten the way they do when she's annoyed with me, which is to say ninety-nine percent of the time.

"What's it for?" I ask again.

"You ask too many questions."

I back away from the bowl that Mama holds out and bump into the refrigerator. I'd crawl in with the dried pork, tofu bricks, and soy milk if it meant getting away from this poison potion. Sighing heavily, Mama shuffles in her slippers to the kitchen table and places the Tonic Soup on my spot, the far right corner. Our lives are arranged according to feng shui, which means that all our furniture is positioned to bring us more luck. Where, may I ask, is this good fortune? I've been sitting in the relationship area of the table for the past six years, and as far as I can tell, the only relationship I have is with my chair.

That's when I spot Mama's required reading for her favorite subject, Stupid Girls, on my plate. The way other mothers clip recipes, Mama cuts out articles about girls my age who are killed by their drunk-driving boyfriends, slain by jilted lovers, and stalked by Internet weirdos after foolishly flirting with them online. Great, just serve up a side order of fear with that Tonic Soup, why don't you, Mama?

"Eat," orders Mama. The hair along her forehead is frizzier than normal from bending over the foul broth. Her cheeks are flushed red. And as usual, she's wearing one of my old junior high school cast-off sweatshirts. I can only hope that no one I know will see her when she goes grocery shopping the way she normally does on Saturday mornings before she locks herself in her bedroom to finish a client's payroll.

"Hey, maybe it'll make you shrink," says Abe, offering up a feeble grin to me.

He's still by the back door, like if he steps into the kitchen, his stomach will lose its contents. But his suggestion opens new possibilities. I stare at the steam snaking off the soup and wonder, Is the Tonic Soup supposed to make me smarter? Nicer? More beautiful now that I'm supposed to be Taiwanese boy bait? Or maybe, just maybe, grow a bra size or two? For that, I'd drink vats of Tonic Soup.

But Mama can hoard secrets, never doling out answers to any of my questions. Especially the ones about Daddy. When I was working on our family tree for a second-grade project, all I got out of her was a *hunh* of annoyance and a mini-lecture that I was so lucky that Daddy was MIF, Missing In Family. Which is how I'm going to end up if she keeps pushing this soup onto me.

Now she slips a couple of fried eggs onto Abe's plate. "Eat," Mama commands us both. Her look is so forbidding, we both shuffle to the table. As much as I want to ignore the article next to my bowl of soup, I can't help reading it like a gawker passing a three-car pileup on a highway, eyes drawn to the carnage. This time, a girl got bludgeoned by her boyfriend last night. Mama underlined the choicer bits.

Not one to pass up such a ripe opportunity to lecture me, Mama taps the article. "See? Be friends first. Take long time to know person. Make sure he Good One." Her lip curls. "This boy Bad One."

Distinctly greener now, Abe pushes the eggs around on his plate. I hear him swallow hard, but I'm too immersed in my own misery to help him out. Besides, I'm busy poking my white porcelain spoon suspiciously at the tiny black orbs bobbing near the soup's surface. I consider bringing the unidentifiable floating objects into my last chemistry class tomorrow and asking Mrs. McAllister what she thinks they are. But then again, I doubt she or any of my teachers have ever stepped a single lily-white, Ked-sneakered foot into one of those apothecary stores that populate the International District. The ones that are filled from floor to ceiling with large dusty jars of dried sea horses and other ground-up, petrified animals.

Under Mama's watchful eyes and Abe's queasy ones, I take a tiny sip. Thankfully, I have a stomach of steel, because the broth is so bitter, it vacuums out my mouth.

"I'm full," I say and push the bowl away from me. "I'm going to do some homework at Janie's house."

Out of the corner of my eye, I try to see if the Homework word has its desired effect on Mama. It doesn't.

"Eat." Mama pushes the bowl back toward me.

"You eat it," I say.

As soon as the words leave my mouth, I wish I could paddle across the sound waves and harpoon what I've said. But my words have already washed down the canals of Mama's ears. She frowns, eyes narrowing into slivers so thin they can cut.

I picture a bubble over her head, one with Lecture Number Two formulating: You Are a Disobedient Daughter. Just like the dead girl in the article whose parents begged her to break up with that Bad One, but did she listen?

"Hey, Ma, I'm feeling sick." Abe waves the peace flag.

I should feel grateful that Abe averts both the crisis and a lecture. But when Mama scurries over to Abe, hand on his forehead like he's a little kid, all I feel is a hangover from binging on bitter hot jealousy.

How could she not know that the reason why he's sick is because he snuck out of the house last night and drank until he couldn't see straight? If it had been me, moaning and groaning in my corner of the table, Mama would have stared right through me, told me to stop acting and given me a list of chores to do. Cinder-yella, that's me.

But Abe is, I realize, and always will be, the eldest son, the beloved Honest Abe, the Golden Child who looks like Mama.

"You go back to bed." Mama fusses and clears his plate for him.

The poor invalid hobbles back up the stairs without a backward glance. Mama follows, clucking after him.

My throat feels burned raw, as though I've already drunk a bowl of bitterness. So I hardly notice the taste when I choke it down, alone.

# 5 ○ Othering

One hundred eighty-seven steps separate my home from Janie's. But a gulf as wide as the South China Sea splits our worlds apart. Guess who's the yippy-skippy escapee from the side inhabited with a lecture-spitting dragon?

I practically sprint to Janie's place I'm so happy to be free of Mama. Like always, I can't wait to cross through Janie's arbor, my gateway to the West. Today, the only Truth Statement I want to hear is the one about last night's flinging: who got trashed and who just talked trash, who went all the way and who didn't. Unless it had anything to do with Mark. Then a couple of white lies would do instead of a blow-by-blow account of how he romanced his date.

"My mom's trying to poison me," I announce to Janie as soon as she opens her blue front door. A bad color, according to Mama and her feng shui books, because they might as well be washing out all their good luck.

Janie's what people once might have called a "healthy" girl, only she's overweight by Lincoln High's anorexic standards, where a size four is considered gargantuan. Having curves in all the wrong places doesn't stop Janie from dressing the way she wants, which usually means miniskirts and cowboy boots, regardless of the season. Today's no different.

Janie reaches up to give me a sympathetic hug, but rears back with a funny expression. Her grin vanishes and all I'm left with is the mirage of her blue braces glinting in the sun.

"I can tell," she says with the brutal honesty of a best friend since third grade. Janie grimaces. "Your breath stinks!"

"Sorry," I mutter, covering my Mama-poisoned breath with my hand.

"Omigod, what weird Chinesey thing is your mom doing to you now?" Janie's big, green eyes are on high beam as she stares at me from under her mass of tight brown curls.

"Who knows, who cares?" I shrug off the small feeling that I'm betraying Mama as Janie pulls me inside Spa Blanco. Like I need any encouragement. I could have pranced into her gleaming, shining, uncluttered house. In the marble-floored foyer, I automatically start to kick off my sneakers, only to remember to leave them on instead of at the door the way we do at House Ho.

The scent of grilled cheese is perfume to my Tonic Soup–assaulted nose. Right on cue, Janie's mom calls from the kitchen, "Great, Patty, you're just in time for lunch."

"And just in time to hear about the dance," says Janie, striding toward the kitchen. "I wouldn't tell my mom a thing until you came."

Even with oozing, melting cheese beckoning, I pause in the middle of the living room. Good-bye, red walls. Hello, suburban beige. A dilapidated fishing basket on the coffee table overflows with blue-gray river rocks where only a week ago red-pillared candles burned.

"What happened to Morocco?" I ask.

"We're *Wabi-Sabi* this week," says Janie.

"Wabi-what?"

"You know, Japanese shabby chic?"

I shake my head.

"Apparently, the red walls made everything else look muddy." Janie rolls her eyes like she's got the world's weirdest mom for being an interior decorator who falls in and out of love with colors. Let's not talk about weirdest moms, shall we? But then it occurs to me that Mama has the Red Wall effect on people: she makes everyone else seem normal.

Janie's (normal) mom is in the kitchen, rereading her well-earmarked *Men Are from Mars, Women Are from Venus* while stirring a pot of soup. Her tiny waist is cinched in one of the 1940s aprons she makes from vintage fabrics and patterns, scoured from flea markets and the Internet.

"Quick, Sharon, we need to detox Patty," says Janie.

If Mama had been with me, she would have breathed out — *hunh!* — at Janie for calling her mother by her first name. That alone would have been enough to launch into Lecture Number Three (Disrespectful Daughter), as if by lecturing me, she would be lecturing Janie by proxy.

"Really?" Sharon's lips quirk up, amused the way she always is when I tell her about the Chinesey things Mama does. After all, she is Mrs. Rationality who told Janie and me to use our heads the summer we thought Janie's bedroom was haunted. So explain to me again how a breeze could have opened Janie's door when we had locked it on purpose so that her little sisters couldn't interrupt our séance?

"Mama took me to see some crazy old lady last night who reads fortunes." Again, I brush off the niggling feeling that

I'm being disloyal to Mama. "She told my mom that I needed to drink this soup or something."

"That is *so* Chinese," says Janie, as if that's a bad thing. As if I'm *not* so Chinese myself. I feel vaguely offended, but I'm more relieved that she sees me as unlike Mama that it washes away any irritation.

*Amen,* I think, but say, "I know," like I'm just as weirded out as Janie is.

"Don't go overboard on drinking *that* soup." Instead, Sharon stirs *her* all-American, good-for-you tomato soup. "I don't think the FDA has totally approved Chinese herbs."

"Trust me, I won't," I promise.

For a split second, I half-wish that Sharon would tell Mama that, too. But I don't dare suggest it because Sharon just might. She had, after all, bought me a training bra back in seventh grade when Mama refused to waste her hard-earned money on something I clearly didn't need. Still don't, if you want the Honest Abe truth, but I'm not about to go around with nipple pokage under my T-shirts.

"So, how was It?" I ask Janie as we sit down to a table with color-coordinated plates and napkins, so different from my hodgepodge home.

The "It" in question only makes Janie shrug, but Sharon, a glutton for any high school gossip, echoes, "Yes, how was It?"

"Great, until Mark and Lindsey were kicked out for getting it on, on the dance floor. It was disgusting."

When the only dates I go on with Mark are in my head, the last image I need hardwired there is of him entwined with someone else. I try to shove Lindsey out of my head: *Bye-bye, bimbo.* It doesn't work. She and her rah-rah baby blues are there to stay.

Janie slurps a huge mouthful of soup, which would have harmonized in my kitchen where conversations routinely take place at the same time as chewing. But in this stainless steel kitchen, only Immaculate Conversation is allowed, and Sharon looks horrified.

"Janie!" Sharon tuts, shooting her a meaningful look while dabbing her own mouth with a napkin.

"What? I'm starving," says Janie, but she wipes her droplets away. "You know, I didn't want to make a pig of myself at dinner."

What is with this eat-like-a-bird in the company of boys? I mean, do guys really think that girls subsist on their conversation when we eat in their presence? I take an extra-large bite out of my sandwich and nearly need to use the international symbol for choking.

Janie laughs with me, her own cheeks bulging with grilled cheese. But her next remark is so salacious, Sharon forgets to remind us of our manners: "Oh! Lindsey and Anne Wong wore the *same* dress."

"You're kidding!" Scandalized, Sharon's eyes widen at this Revenge of the Wallflower moment: how the Queen Bee of the Proud Crowd wouldn't budge out of her chair for the first hour because the Statewide Spelling Bee Champ was buzzing around the dance floor in the same dress.

While Janie and Sharon dissect the matching red dresses — such a winter color for a spring dance, no? — I'm fuming because I wanted to go to the Spring Fling. Badly. So what if the only shopping scenario I could imagine was Mama scouring the sales racks until she found a sea-foam green dress marked down seventy percent because no one could look remotely human in it.

I don't realize I've sighed until Sharon puts one perfectly manicured hand on top of mine.

"You'll go to dances one day, too," Sharon tells me firmly. "These high school boys might not appreciate your unique looks, but trust me, someday, someone will."

"Uh-huh," I say, trying not to dwell on how her words make it sound like I'm going to need a miracle for "someone" to appreciate my "unique looks" someday in the way off, very distant future.

"And really, it's not like you missed anything big," says Janie.

I doubt that very much, but say brightly, "There's always Homecoming next year. I think I'm allowed to go to dances now."

"That's great!" Sharon pushes away her half-full plate like a couple of naked spinach leaves could stuff her and squeezes my hand. "Watch out, Lincoln High."

"Just Taiwanese guys."

"But your mother married a white man," says Sharon, who exchanges a bewildered look with Janie. Their eyebrows lift like a double set of parentheses fencing in their not-so-private thoughts: Mrs. Ho is *so* Chinese. I decide I better keep math camp to myself because that would confirm that I'm *so* Chinese, too.

"Yeah," chimes in Janie. "So how come you can't date white guys? What's with that?"

I shake my head like the answer is a mystery to me, too, when the truth is so clear, it could be lit up with a blinking, neon sign. The only mistake Mama ever admits to is marrying my white guy of a dad. So the chances of me dating a white guy are the same as me squirming out of math camp:

zero. But how do I explain that to a girl who dishes with her mother about boys and birth control?

"So, who does that leave?" asks Janie. Her smile gleams with possibility. "Dylan Nguyen."

Dylan Nguyen is a junior with such a bad case of acne, he makes my complexion look flawless. But Sharon nods like this makes perfect sense, like this is the inevitable, logical solution. Like dating a white guy is totally out of the realm of my possibility. After all, canaries of a feather flock together.

Newsflash: this canary wants to fly solo.

"He's Vietnamese," I tell them.

They exchange befuddled looks again and Sharon mumbles something about splitting hairs. What they don't know is that Mama can parse the finest strand of hair into a thousand clearly delineated pieces.


After I go for a long, hard run, I return to a House Ho that still stinks of Tonic Soup. Really, one does wonder whether that soup is Mama's attempt to keep boys away from me. As if my "unique looks" really merit that extreme measure.

"You finish homework?" Mama asks by way of greeting me, her fingers still click-click-clicking on her ten-key calculator while she scans a ledger, not sparing me a glance. Files are spread all over the dining table, an avalanche of accounts. It must be quarterly reporting time for her clients.

"Just about," I say and hurry into the kitchen to fix dinner before she finds out that my homework accounting isn't reconciling. Homework to do does not equal homework done.

Safe in my bedroom after stir-frying noodles for everyone, and yes, guzzling down bowl two of Tonic Soup, I flop on my bed only to have my head hit a book instead of my pillow. Lifting up, I slide out Mama's favorite read, Gavin de Becker's *Protecting the Gift*. The same woman who comparison shops for everything had run to the bookstore to pay full price for this hardback book after the author, a security guru, talked on *Oprah* about the creeps and crazies who prey on women and children. I interpret this light bedtime read as permission to whack a geek where it counts if he tries to seduce me with an equation at math camp.

Ironically, the book about protecting yourself looks battleworn, wearing Mama's sticky notes like bandages. I set it gently on my bedside table and wander to my desk. The call of geometry can't be denied any longer — procrastinated again, can you stand it?

At midnight, I escape math and tiptoe downstairs to make some tea to settle my upset stomach.

Two doses of Mama's Tonic Soup + (Sharon's grilled cheese sandwich + my lactose intolerance) = gastronomical mistake of peptic proportions.

The dining room lights are on, which isn't weird given that Mama is a late-to-bed, early-to-riser who thinks sleep is for the weak, not for the weary. What *is* weird is Mama using a huge pile of spreadsheets as a pillow, one hand on her big calculator and the other grazing her laptop computer. Her hangnailed fingers twitch like she's trying to crunch numbers even in her sleep.

Part of me wants to wake Mama, lead her to her bedroom, take off her tiny slippers and tuck her in. But I know that once her eyes are open, Mama will dose herself with some exceptionally strong, highly caffeinated green tea and keep toiling until her clients' receipts reconcile their bank statements, not one penny misplaced. Her persistence and fiscal fluency is why clients overlook her broken English. It's how she's paying for Harvard. And summer camp.

Guilt, more substantial than any of her lectures could produce, bloats my heart. I pad softly to the living room and grab a pilled-up crocheted afghan, one with so many snags that Janie's mother would have incinerated it on sight. When I drape it carefully over Mama, her thin shoulders lift in a soft sigh.

"It's OK, Mama," I murmur and her face relaxes. Not exactly into a smile, but close enough to approximate satisfaction.

Before I dim the light, I drink in Mama's expression, the way I wish she'd look at me when we're both awake.

# 6 ∘ Nipping

Bowl number sixteen of Tonic Soup starts my very last day as a freshman with a kick. Call me vain, but since camouflaging my bad breath with peppermint is a matter of social-life-or-death, I opt to brush my teeth three more times. I can still taste Tonic Soup. So I gargle with Listermint. And I miss the bus. Which means that Mama is driving foul-mouthed me to school.

Even before my hand is on the car door, my annoyed chauffeur is *hunh*-ing at me. As much as I'm tempted to negotiate with Mama — you lay off the Tonic Soup, and I won't need to gargle and brush for ten extra minutes — I refrain. Risking Lecture Number Four (I Do Everything for You) seems hardly worth ruining the happiest day of every freshman's life. As of 3:05 this afternoon, we're sophomores.

So I sit quietly, hunched down in my seat in hopes that Mama will forget about me. Fat chance of that when we approach her new client's office, the doctor she's visiting this morning to organize his badly disarrayed bills. An especially loud *hunh* is aimed at me. It's raining, and my hair is going to get soaked, but I can't take this irradiation by irritation a moment longer. We're just a quarter mile from school. So I tell Mama, "You can just let me off here. I'll walk the rest of the way."

Mama glances at her watch and her lips tighten with annoyance. Heaven forbid, Ho Mei-Li is a second late to crunch numbers. Without putting up the least bit of resistance to my suggestion, Mama swerves into the parking lot, as she orders me, "Hurry! No late!"

Naturally, I slowpoke along on the sidewalk until I'm past glaring distance. And then I hustle to school, grumbling to myself about Torture by Tonic Soup. I'm trying to figure out a way to convince Abe that the soup builds lean muscle mass (his goal in life), when a familiar Neanderthal grunts, "Yo, Nip!"

I keep walking, head down as I'm caught in a storm of why's. Why now? Why today, the last day of school? Ku Klux Kosanko has pretty much left me alone since Abe and his baseball buddies had a "chat" with him at the beginning of the year for harassing me.

But a car slows down, way down.

"Chopsticks, I'm talking to you," taunts Steve Kosanko. His voice has an edge to it like I should be prostrating myself in front of him. Out of my periphery, I can see his huge forehead and a thick unibrow. "Maybe Half-breed Ho no speak English."

*No, Idiot,* I respond in my head as I walk a little faster. *It's just that I don't speak Stupid.*

Steve's cackle follows me. I can smell his hate the way you can always smell your yard after it's become some dog's personal outhouse.

Remind me again why I insisted on walking the rest of the way to school? I'd kick myself except then I'd probably trip, and I'm determined to walk like I don't hear Steve nipping at my heels with his racist pig comments.

"Fung, twung, wung, low hung."

And here I thought time was supposed to mature us all. Obviously, Steve is stuck in some kind of elementary school time warp, proving that once an imbecile, always an imbecile. Another round of jeering laughter washes over me like mud. Steve's voice deepens to a leer: "Wanna check me out, Ho? Free, looky, looky."

I hike my backpack higher onto my shoulders as if my books and papers could shield me. *Say something,* I yell at myself. *Don't take his crap.* But if words can't hurt you, how can they help you?

My eyes race up and down driveways, hunting for a good escape route. The huge "Lincoln High, Home of the Patriots" sign is up ahead. But I don't want to give Steve the satisfaction of seeing me bolt. *Just ignore him,* Mama would tell me. As if *that* ever works. Ignoring Steve just makes him madder that he can't screw with my head.

Against my better judgment, I look over at Steve, hanging out the driver's side window like the dog he is: a pit bull, ugly and mean. I may have x'ed Steve Kosanko out of every yearbook picture he's ever spoiled, but I'll never forget how mean his eyes can look. He's shorter than I am, but outweighs me by a good fifty pounds. All muscular upper arms and skinny legs that don't look like they can sprint. Trust me, he can. He got enough practice on me in grade school.

When I first complained about Steve, my fourth-grade teacher, Mr. Enoch, just patted me on the head and said, "He's got a crush on you." Right, more like he wanted to crush me. My fifth-grade teacher gave me a look like *Come on, what can this puny kid do to you?* Well, nothing except turn school into a three-season hunting ground for Patty Ho.

But then Abe morphed into Lincoln's all-star pitcher with a team of he-men friends. Friends who enjoyed pounding on bullies. Friends who let Steve know I was off-limits. Friends who are graduating.

Before I know what Steve's planning, before I can dodge out of the firing line, he rears back and spits. A giant glob lands on my cheek and slides down, sluggy tears. All the voices inside me — the strident one telling me to get my ass in gear and stand up for myself, the mousy one whispering to haul my ass out of here — are speechless.

My feet are rooted into the sidewalk. I can't move.

Then my heart hardens into a pellet of disbelief as I stare at the guy sitting in the passenger's seat. Mark Scranton, lust object since sixth grade when he moved into my neighborhood and my heart. The guy whose voice I can pick out in the most raucous soccer game. The guy whose campaign speech I wrote.

*Et tu,* Mark?

Mr. Class President won't meet my eyes. And I won't stop staring. Finally, Steve's car peels down the street, leaving fart fumes. And only then do I wipe my cheek on my sleeve.

# 7 ∘ Changing

Shielding my spit-stained face behind my long hair, I speed walk to my locker. All I can think about is changing. Changing schools so I don't have to deal with Steve Kosanko next year. Changing lives so I never have to face Mark again.

This morning, I settle for changing clothes.

Thankfully, I don't run into anyone because I don't think I can manage a "hello" or "sorry" without breaking apart, and I don't want *that* to get back to Steve Kosanko.

I reach my locker. For one long, Alzheimer's moment, I can't remember my combination. When I finally do, I paw through a year's worth of high school detritus: notes from Janie and Laura, empty potato chip bags, a couple of lint-covered gummy bears, crumpled quizzes. I almost lose it when I find a picture of me and Mark that slipped to the back of my locker, snapped at his house after we practiced his campaign speech, the one that I wrote for him, the one that he passed off as his own. I would tear the picture up into a million pieces, but I'm on a mission now.

I shove aside my biology book, and at last dredge up the oversized, orange T-shirt, left over from a couple of weeks ago when I wasted my time painting a "Make Our Mark! Vote Scranton!" campaign banner. Who would have known that it would be *my* cheek that would carry his friend's wet mark?

The bell rings, lockers clang shut, and kids race to class. I'm usually part of the student herd, but today I head to the girls' bathroom. Luckily, it's empty.

The damp spot on my sleeve, left from wiping Steve's spit off my face, is drying, but I'd rather break out worse than Dylan Nguyen than keep this spitrag on for another minute. I don't even bother with a stall. Instead, I yank off my brand-new shirt and drop it onto the sticky bathroom floor. On the wall is a flyer for last week's junior prom. The day after Janie's boyfriend asked her to go with him, she went shopping for The Perfect Prom Dress with her mom. I prescribed The Perfect Prom Therapy for myself and blew the last of my Chinese New Year lucky money on this red shirt.

Can you say, "Buyer's remorse"?

The freebie T-shirt I got for running the Sound to Narrows 12K race with my cross-country team hangs loose and falls past my thighs. Not a good look, I'm sure. A glimpse of myself in the mirror confirms that, but as I look at my reflection, I wonder what it is that makes Steve hate me so much. Sure, my hair is more black than brown, and my eyes have a slight almond tilt to them. But my teeth are as white as snow, and half of me is just the same as him, Mark and 99.98 percent of my high school. So why does being part-Taiwanese make me all-disgusting in Steve's eyes?

My right cheek hurts from all my scrubbing, but I can't stop squirting more soap into my hand and lathering again.

The cold water makes my teeth clench, but I splash until my whole face feels numb.

Here's the thing: no matter how much I scrub, no matter if my skin is rubbed raw, no matter how much cover-up and concealer I wear, I can't erase who I am. I feel like I'm stuck on some infinite teeter-totter: too-white, too-Asian; too-white, too-Asian. As much as I try to balance in the middle, I keep getting slammed, from one side to the other.

Against my pale, cold skin, my eyes look darker than ever. I finally ask myself the question that hurts the most: How could Mark have joined Steve's hate-spewing squad? Save getting a lobotomy, how am I ever going to forget the sight of him, driving away like he had no idea what Steve had just done to me?

I turn away from the mirror. Running my red shirt in the washing machine a hundred times in a row, fading it to pink, would never salvage it. It's stained forever, marinating in the memory of Steve Kosanko and his scummy new sidekick, Mark Scranton. I pull the photo of me and Mark out of my back pocket, feeling like I'm going to throw up as I look at his face, no longer gorgeous, but gross. I crumple Mark in my hand and flush him down the toilet.

Mama would have had a conniption about the colossal waste of forty bucks if she saw me tossing my ruined shirt into the garbage. That would surely have brought on Lecture Number Five: You So Wasteful.

But I don't look back.

**The halls in between** classes are usually a no-geeks-land as the exceptionally brainy and fashion-challenged hurry to avoid being picked on.

I wish I could stay out here in the quiet where I can see forever down the hall. But this is a no-girls-land, no matter who she is, because Mr. Allen, the vice-principal, is waddling out of a classroom, heading straight toward me. He looks like a beluga whale, in the same puffy, white, harmless way.

"Patty, anything wrong?" he asks, concerned.

This is one of the times when being part-Asian works to my advantage. Mr. Allen takes one look at me and sees only what he expects to see from a girl whose last name is Ho: a studious Asian kid. He assumes that I have a perfectly acceptable reason for being late. Part of me wants to pretend that I was up to no good: *Nope, just looking for a safe place to get high, thank you very much.*

When it comes down to it, what can this beluga whale do when just yesterday he was the one who clapped the great white Steve Kosanko shark on the back and handed him the student citizenship award for the second year in a row? He was the one who announced to the whole school that Mark won the election.

"All righty then. Better head to class," Mr. Allen says, lumbering away and expecting the silent Asian girl standing alone in the hall to follow his directions. I hear and obey.


I drift into Honors English late. Mrs. Meyers is leaning against the blackboard, legs crossed like she's at a bar, just chatting with some friends. She scans my ice-numb face and her gaze drops down to my T-shirt. A question instantly formulates in her eyes. I may not be the most fashion aware, but I know better than to wear a too-big, orange T-shirt listing corporate sponsors unless I'm outside, sweating from running or biking. I have become my mother, whose fashion sense is: the cheaper the better, but free is best.

Worse, I can feel Mark scrutinizing me, but when I glare at him, dare him to look at me straight in my face, his eyes fall to his hands, twisted on his desk. And this, ladies and gentlemen, is our future leader of America.

"Everything OK, Patty?" asks Mrs. Meyers.

I nod and plaster an A-OK smile on my face even though I don't think I'll B-OK for a while. As I slide into my seat, Janie whispers, "What happened to you?"

I take one look at Janie with her pink miniskirt and funky cowboy boots and chubby thighs. She can complain all day long about being fat, but her extra fifteen pounds don't stop her from getting dates, don't stop her from fitting in, don't stop her from being normal. By virtue of blotchy red skin that is still white when it counts, she doesn't get spit upon. Jealousy scrambles sure-footed into my heart.

Her forehead-wrinkling half-smile of support makes me ashamed of my Janie-envy. This is my best friend, after all.

"He spit on me," I mutter to Janie, as I pass up my English composition book. I don't have to tell her who the "he" is. "And Mark was with him."

Janie's solidarity is immediate, never mind that she's had a not-so-secret crush on Mark for the past two years, too, not that I've ever admitted my own stupid infatuation. She screws up her face in disgust. Without any hesitation, she swivels in her seat, facing Mark, and mouths: "Asshole loser."

We can glare all we want at him, but there's nothing any-one can do about the real loser. Not when Steve's mother is on the school board. Not when the last time I lodged a com-plaint, my junior high school principal, Mrs. Stark, just hemmed and hawed and said she'd look into it. What she meant was she was looking into her future as a principal.

"Some of my favorite reads, perfect for keeping your brain sharp this summer," says Mrs. Meyers, back to business. Normally, I'm all ears in Honors English, totally absorbed because Mrs. Meyers talks to us like peers, not kids. Her hand floats across the chalkboard, but her writing could have been Sanskrit for all its wriggles in front of my unseeing eyes.

"I loved *The Corrections*," cries Anne, ever the dedicated Asian student even on this last day of school when all the grades have been calculated. I want to shake her: You are the reason why everyone hates us. Why everyone calls the two of us the Asian Mafia even though only one of us dominates every class discussion. Guess which one? God, Anne, why do you have to raise the curve? Why can't you stay quiet like me?

Mrs. Meyers hefts a huge cardboard box onto her desk. Her hands are on either side of the box, like she's protecting its contents. "Now the day you've been waiting for. I can honestly say that I enjoyed reading every one of your Truth Statements." She picks a couple off the top of the stack. Thick binders. Laminated covers. Professional bindings.

I feel like my lungs have collapsed. On the Monday they were due, Mrs. Meyers gave us an extension until three in the afternoon to turn in our Truth Statements, a special dispensation because of the Spring Fling. I hadn't seen anyone else's work. Until now. Hadn't we all moaned about how behind we were on writing our Truth Statements?

Talk about truth is cheap. The whole truth was that everyone — except me — went full-throttle for the A+.

Mrs. Meyers beams, proud mama who gave birth to all these overachievers. "Most of you are ready to write spectacular, honest college applications. Just remember, dig deep inside yourself to find the real answers. The real truth." Then Mrs. Meyers starts calling up people to collect their Truth Tomes from her. "Anne."

The front of Anne's three-inch binder is decorated with a collage, rice paper decoupaged with photographs of a traditional Chinese garden moongate. Geez, even if she listed all her spelling bee trophies and math championships and geography ribbons, they couldn't have filled an entire binder, could they?

"Mark," calls Mrs. Meyers.

The Class Coward shuffles up to claim his binder-clipped ream of paper, at least fifty pages thick. Too bad he keeps his eyes averted from the blasts of disgust coming from my desk. I'd bet every one of my favorite books and Janie's entire wardrobe that there isn't so much as a single sentence in Mark's Truth Statement that says he's friends with a racist pig. Or that he's too much of a wimp to stop Steve Kosanko from spewing on me.

A shimmer of pink diverts my attention from The Traitor. Janie, who triple-spaced and wide-margined last year's world history report, holds a dossier with a pink cover sheet tied together with a sparkly silver ribbon. I stare at her work, betrayed again. Hadn't she been stressing about this assignment as much as I had?

*Come on, people,* I want to shout. *We've been alive for about fifteen years. How much truth could any of us accumulate?*

My paltry three pages are such a weak excuse of a Truth Statement that I'm the only one without mine back at the end of the class. Anne doesn't miss this fact, projecting in her loud voice as if we're at dim sum and need to talk over the chattering Chinese and rolling carts: "Where's Patty's?"

"The only truth we need to know is that her shirt is butt ugly." Cole laughs, nothing but good-natured humor. His grubby concert T-shirts never look any better than what I have on, and everyone knows it.

I smile faintly. "That's the god-awful truth."

"Right on," says Cole.

"Patty wrote the truth," Janie says, wrenching around in her desk to stare pointedly at Mark. "Did everybody else?"

Mark gets out of his hot seat so quickly, he knocks over his Untruth Statement. All his white lies spill onto the floor. He doesn't stop to pick up any of the loose pages, just slinks out of the classroom.

"Mark?" calls Mrs. Meyers. She frowns, confused. Her eyes dart first to Janie and then rest on me.

*Why can't I confront Steve and Mark myself?* Janie, fearless Janie, who says cellulite be damned and wears thigh-high skirts anyway, can. And does.

I duck my head, ashamed of my silence. My hands push in my stomach as if I could dig out the truth, tug it from my belly button.

But the only truth is this: I've demolished my GPA. Next year's class president hates me now. Steve Kosanko is going to be the Grim Reaper of my sophomore year. And a butt ugly shirt can't cover the fact that I'm a coward, no different from Mark.

Why is the truth so hard to swallow?

Apparently, Mrs. Meyers can't swallow my hard, bitter truths either.

"Patty," she says. "I want to see you after class."

# 8 ∘ Incomplete

As the other students pile out of the classroom, I can hear summer vacation lightening their voices. Mrs. Meyers doesn't seem to hear anything, erasing the chalkboard in long, full sweeps, as if cleaning it is the only thing she's thinking about. In my mind, I'm halfway through bleaching my skin before Mrs. Meyers turns to face me, looking as if she knows what I'm doing and doesn't like it.

With a slight frown, Mrs. Meyers picks up a thin, red file folder and heads toward my desk, sitting down in Janie's seat beside mine. She says, "What you wrote is good, very good." Her eyes probe mine, like she can see straight over my Great Wall of Chinese Silence. "Your Truth Statement is stronger than anything you've produced this year."

I nod, *OK,* wondering, so why hasn't she handed me my paper yet?

"But you only wrote half the truth."

"Half?" I repeat.

Mrs. Meyers nods, closes her eyes, and when she opens

them, they're urgent, hot black coals. She hugs the file folder with my writing to her heart before she hands it to me.

When I open the file, my breath escapes in a whoosh, sounding like the air escaping out of a deflating balloon.

Incomplete. Written in bright, red ink. That one damning word is a stake through my broken heart. How did she know? Today, I feel incomplete in too many ways to count. My family, missing one doting father. My half-and-half self. My nonexistent love life, including a newly fractured fantasy. Take it from me; my Truth Statement is the least of my worries.

My tongue stops working, and I stutter, "But, but . . . I th-thought you said this was better than anything I've written."

"It is. And it's more truthful than half of what I read," says Mrs. Meyers, throwing her hand out to take in the entire empty classroom.

"Then why . . ."

"Because you can do better." Mrs. Meyers crosses her arms. "You wrote this in one night."

A pronouncement, not a question. I nod slowly. How can I deny it when that's the God's honest truth?

"Excellent for one night's work." Her smile is admiring, but then she scribbles the words I've seen on my papers all year long. "More. Give me more." Her fingers tap her bottom lip, her forehead wrinkles pensively. "No, what I mean is, give yourself more." She stands up. Even in her heels, I know I must tower over her by a good six inches. Hating to feel gawky, I stay in my seat while Mrs. Meyers returns to erasing the chalkboard, standing on tiptoes to skim the top. "You'll have until the end of the summer to rewrite this."

Good, because when Mama sees the big "I" on my report card, I'll be confined to math camp for the rest of my life. That should be plenty of time to write the Whole Truth.

"Oh, and Patty . . ."

I sigh. What now?

"Mr. Powell told me that you got into math camp in spite of your best efforts." Another amused smile plays on her dark lips. And here I thought that I had done a good job hiding from everyone that I *can* do math. *When* I want.

"Stanford, you know, is nothing like this." This time, Mrs. Meyers gestures with her white chalk to the halls, where I can hear chasing feet and shrill screams. If I close my eyes, I could swear I was still in elementary school. Either that, or this is just one of the nightmares I have before big meets and important tests. "All I'm saying, Patty, is when a door like Stanford opens, run through." Her arms are crooked at her side, tensed like she's going to break into a sprint herself. "You might be surprised to find yourself on the other side."

Great, my Honors English teacher can moonlight as a fortune cookie writer. Like always, I keep my thoughts to myself.

No one must have informed Mr. Powell that today's the last day of school because he jots another geometric proof on the chalkboard. I'm not joking. Then again, he's fairly oblivious, which accounts for his nickname, Mr. Bowel. As in, he's lost in the bowels of math. So it's no big surprise that when kids pass yearbooks to each other to sign, me included, Mr. Powell is still mumbling circuitously with his back to us.

Cole hands me his yearbook, and I write the first thing that pops into my head: "Run through open doors, dude!" Which, I suppose, means that my conversation with Mrs. Meyers has lodged itself in the bowels of my subconscious. Her message must make sense to Cole because he skims my inscription and nods wisely. "Right on," he whispers to me. "Open doors!"

Mr. Powell drones on, adding two new columns on the chalkboard, more proofs about who knows what. For a moment, I zone out, imagining the geekzoids lurking on the other side of my math camp door. Then, on the last clean page of my geometry notebook, I write:

### The Patty Ho Happy Camper Theorem

*Given:* Math camp is a done deal.
*Prove:* It is the open door I'm supposed to run through this summer.

| Statement | Reason |
|---|---|
| 1. I don't have a summer job lined up. | 1. Given. Procrastination, what can I say? |
| 2. All the good jobs are taken now. | 2. Given. Big oops. |
| 3. I want to be far, far away from Mark Scranton . . . | 3. Given!! |
| 4. . . . and Mama's glowering. Therefore, I might as well embrace math camp because it's not like I have anything better to do. | 4. Save me! My excitement is overwhelming. |

If math camp is my open door, why does it feel like I'm being locked away?

At lunch, Laura practically causes a riot when she crashes across the cafeteria, bumping into everyone to get to me. Ever the idealist, Laura looks at me so earnestly, we could have been back in fifth grade, cementing our friendship over a petition to save the rain forest. Which means one thing. Janie's already shared the news of my early morning run-in with Steve. Somehow, I don't know what's more gratifying: that I don't have to retell the story or that Laura looks like she wants to stamp out Steve Kosanko, high school pollutant.

"You've got to tell your brother about Steve Kosanko," Laura declares as we walk to our usual lunch place, third table from the cafeteria's back door. An excellent escape hatch in case I'm caught by Steve on my own.

"If you don't, we will," says Janie, already scanning the lunchroom for Abe.

I shake my head. Belly-button Grandmother doesn't need to tell me what could happen. The headline in the newspaper would read: "Harvard student rejected for fistfight." I couldn't be responsible for that. Geez, then I'd have to live the rest of my life as the Reason for Abe's Failure. Thanks, but being the Disappointing Daughter is tough enough in House Ho.

"School's over in three hours," I tell them. "It's not worth it."

"Then what are you going to do next year? Or this summer?" demands Laura.

According to my Happy Camper Math Theorem, math camp is as good a place as any to run to. Maybe not with my arms spread wide the way Mrs. Meyers wanted me to, but with my eyes wide open. I know what I'm getting myself into. Stanford is 903 miles from Mama, 903 miles from Steve Kosanko and not nearly enough miles from Mark.

That's how I find myself announcing as if I planned this all along instead of Mama, "I'm going to math camp."

"But you don't even like math," says Janie, all confused. "This is another weird Chinesey thing, isn't it?"

No, this is just a weird Patty thing. But I simply shrug, not saying anything at all.

# 9 ∘ Potluck

"Come downstairs!" Mama bellows from the kitchen. "Everybody almost here!"

Another loud clang comes from below, and I wonder, *What on earth could Mama possibly be cooking now?* She's already made enough food to feed the imperial army and besides, isn't the point of a potluck that everyone brings a dish to share?

I walk past Abe's bedroom, plastered with Japanese anime posters featuring doe-eyed girls with impossibly big boobs. He's prone on his bed as if reading comic books has sprained his brain. Let me get this straight. On our first day of summer vacation, I've been mopping, and now he's the one moping?

Earlier, I set the buffet table and polished the windows (as if anyone other than Mama was going to notice whether they were dirty or not) while Mama stewed in the kitchen, muttering about how Mrs. Shang, better known as The Gossip Lady, would just bring Jell-O again to our potluck party. "She's so cheap! I spend twenty dollars on duck and she spend a couple of cents," she grumbled as she poured another can of beer on top of the duck. It ate at Mama, that Jell-O inequity.

Abe sighs and throws his arm dramatically over his eyes.

"What's wrong with *you*?" I have to admit, my pity meter is running on empty. If I had gotten into Harvard and were escaping Mama and memories of Mark, you wouldn't have caught me lolling around, potluck or no potluck.

But, no, Abe moans, "God, why do we have to have a potluck tonight?"

"Oh, poor you," I say, picking a careful path through to him. Catch my room flooding ankle-deep in clothes, and Mama's screeching would have been so loud, banshees would have flocked to her for lessons.

But then I see the gray HARVARD T-shirt, balled up in his right hand. It doesn't take a rocket scientist to put two and two together. This is Mama's hour of glory, proof that no one ever need pity Ho Mei-Li for being the sole unmarried woman in the Potluck Group.

Mama doesn't just want to trot Honest Abe out tonight; she wants him gift-wrapped for everyone to envy, specifically Mrs. Chan, who spent the last seven years bragging about her own son's genius-level IQ, his perfect score on the SAT and his grand master chess status. An hour into Abe's acceptance at Harvard and Stan's rejection, Mama revised history. Lo and behold! Abe was no longer wasting his time with sports; Stan Chan, former Potluck Group pet, wasted his with chess. Faster than Ichiro can steal second base, Abe's baseball trophies were yanked off his desk and displayed prominently on the mantel. Guess who gets to dust them?

So shoot spit-'n'-shine me; I giggle.

Abe's eyes narrow, looking dangerously like Mama's, and he hurls the T-shirt at me. "You wear it then, if you think it's so funny," he bites out.

My hand darts out to grab his T-shirt from the air, a fast reflex response from years of dodging the balls he's thrown at me.

"Sorry, I'm going to Stanford." And with those words, I fall in love with my Stanford card. It strikes Abe speechless.

The doorbell rings, and Abe and I look at each other in dread, reunited partners in misery. His head flops back onto his pillow; I want to flop onto the floor like a spineless jelly-fish. When I was nine, I figured out the Potluck equation: one night of potluck bragging equals four days of parental nagging. "How come you not read *Pride and Prejudice* like Emily?" or "How come you not get A+ in science like Stan?"

Tonight would be different.

Mama was singing to the tune of "O, Harvard Mia," an aria she wrote and practiced daily over the past four months.

"Showtime," I say, floating Abe's T-shirt on top of his face and hustling out of his bedroom before he can clobber me. I hear a ball bouncing off the back of his door as it slams shut.

For the first time since Belly-button Grandmother prescribed Tonic Soup, our house is filled with fragrant scents. Beer duck, *mapo tofu,* stir-fried rice vermicelli noodles. While all the kids are feasting in the family room, the parents in the living room are eating morsels of Mama's pride and joy, meticulously prepared, generously sized and Harvard-filled.

To Mama's vast disappointment, the Chans, better known as The Wise Guys for having such a smart-ass kid, called earlier, saying that Stan had caught the flu. More like a bad case of Family Shame. But I couldn't blame the Chans. Being compared to Abe for fourteen years has been an effective diet

for my self-esteem, whittling it down to chopstick-thin proportions. Who'd suffer a starvation diet like that willingly, for
even a single evening?

As if The Gossip Lady overheard my thoughts, she shrieks
with laughter. Name any Asian person within a fifty-mile radius, and Mrs. Shang can dredge up some juicy tidbit, usually embarrassing like when she told everyone that Mr. Chu
had been fired after working in the same high-tech company
for twenty-two years. Soon after that bit of news traveled from
her mouth to our ears, the Chus dropped out of The Potluck
Group. While we don't see them anymore, The Gossip Lady
makes sure we're kept current on their affairs.

We kids glance uneasily at each other because, given different circumstances, it could be one of us that the parents are
laughing about. Once, we posted an eavesdropper near the
adults who were playing a ruthless game of My Kid Is Better
Than Yours.

"Mrs. Shang just said that Emily made it to first chair in
the symphony," the eavesdropper reported. "The youngest
first chair in five years."

"Wow," Emily said, looking shocked. "Mama said I took
too long to make it to first chair."

The rest of us glared at Emily, not because we were jealous
of her so much as we dreaded the post-potluck lecturing: "If
you practiced violin harder, you could be like Emily. You
practice two hours tomorrow."

There are four families and nine kids in The Potluck Group.
One lucky one, Emily the Virtuoso, has already escaped to
college. Sitting across the living room from me are her little
sisters, the China Dolls. They're identical twins a year older

than me whose claim to potluck fame is their glossy, jet black hair and porcelain skin. My whitened skin gets no such looks of envy. I've cheated by adding white to my gene pool whereas the China Dolls are pure-breeds, superior for producing such light skin on their own.

They are doing an extreme makeover on The Baby, the three-year-old who just started Saturday morning Chinese school, poor *bo-po-mo-fo* thing. They've already painted her fingernails, and have moved on to her toes. I tuck my long, bare feet under my legs. My feet are at least twice the size of the China Dolls' tiny ones. Before anyone arrived tonight, I stashed my size ten sandals in the closet so I wouldn't hear their "*Wow!* Patty, your shoes are so big!" when they placed their child-sized ones next to my dragon boats the way they usually do.

With a few deft twists of The Baby's wispy hair, the China Dolls convert *Mei-Mei* into Bebe, complete with a sophisticated up-do. In less than five minutes, The Baby accomplishes what I haven't been able to do in six years: be inducted into the China Doll private sorority, an exclusive club only for the petite, beautiful and all-Asian.

"This would have been cute for the last school dance," says China Doll One, taking The Baby's hand and twirling her around.

China Doll Two looks at me curiously. "What did you wear to yours?"

They are so lucky, those China Dolls. Their dad is a second-generationer, meaning he was born in America. The fallout of that good luck is that the China Dolls can wear makeup, dress in the latest fashions, and even hear a compliment or two straight from his mouth, if not their mom's. It's why the China Dolls have such, shall we say, healthy self-esteems.

While I try to figure out a way to be honest yet save face, I look away to where Anne is studying a math book, not paying attention to what the China Dolls are doing to her baby sister. What a geek-and-a-half. School's over, summer's begun. But even Anne somehow convinced her first-generation parents to let her go to a school dance with some hunk from another school. So that makes me a double geek. I've never even been asked.

"I didn't go," I mumble, reaching new lows on the Social Scale.

"Really?" shrieks China Doll Two so loud, she could have gone vocal cord to vocal cord with her mom, The Gossip Lady. "But Mama told us that you can go to dances now."

"Yeah, but only with Taiwanese guys."

"But you're white!" says China Doll One.

My cheeks flame. Whatever whiteness there is on my skin burns to a crisp. I am too white to be one of the China Dolls, not white enough for Steve Kosanko.

China Doll One giggles. "Well, we can only date Taiwanese guys, too, right, Grace?"

"Right," says China Doll Two, grinning secretively at her twin.

Anne, the other outcast shunned from the China Dolls Club for her flat seaweed hair and stumpy legs, looks up from her math book. "I think Asian guys are cute."

At this, China Doll One snorts. "Like, when have you ever dated an Asian guy?"

"Like, when have you?" asks Anne.

Panic wrinkles the China Dolls' foreheads, making them look like overgrown Shar-Pei puppies. Had they known lines pleated their precious skin, the China Dolls would have sprinted home in their tiny sandals to slather on a mud mask. China Doll Two demands, "How do you know?"

"Know what?" I ask.

"Duh! They date white guys," says Anne.

"White guys?" I blurt out. Instantly, my heart shrinks a couple of sizes as I remember my white guy who betrayed me.

"Shhh!" The China Dolls cast anxious looks at the living room, where all the parents are sitting, blissfully ignorant of the white-guy dating that's gone on under their flat noses. No matter what generation our parents are, the most important mandate in their lives is to marry us girls off to a "good one." Good, of course, meaning a rich Taiwanese man.

"Duh! Add two and two together." Anne scowls at me like I'm the first half-witted, part-Asian twit she's encountered in her life. "God, you really need our math camp, don't you?"

*Our* math camp?

*Our?* As in hers and mine?

That tidbit of information isn't lost on the China Dolls either. They stare at me as if my IQ jumped a full thirty points. China Doll One asks, "You're going to math camp?"

China Doll Two whispers, "Where?"

"Stanford," answers their mother. Mrs. Shang charges into the family room with her gossip-sensing nose twitching in the air. Everything about this woman is wide — hips, nose and mouth.

I can tell by the way the China Dolls tilt forward on the

orange sofa that their panic is mounting as they try to detect whether their mom — she of the bionic ears — overheard their white guy revelation. Lucky for them, Mrs. Shang is looking at me greedily. I know she wishes she could steal my one potluck-worthy accomplishment and wing it to her son who's upstairs with Abe, playing computer games. "Your mama just told us. So maybe you go to Stanford for college, right?"

I mumble something incomprehensible about college being three years away, hoping Mrs. Shang will find something else to gossip about.

"You kids want?" Mrs. Shang holds out her Jell-O, green this time.

The China Dolls shake their heads, not because of their obsessive weight watching (God forbid they break the three-digit pound barrier), but because their stomachs are full of envy for me. Me, Mama's disappointment of a daughter. Me, the too-white girl who will never be part of the exclusive China Doll club. Me, the newly dubbed math wizard who hasn't stepped one big foot onto the Stanford campus. It's dizzying that all those self-help books that Janie and her mother devour are right: perception is everything.

"How could you do this to us?" wails China Doll One as soon as their mother marches back to gossip with the adults.

"Now all we're going to hear this summer is how you and Anne are going to get into Stanford!" cries China Doll Two.

"It's not fair," they repeat like broken dolls.

Stanford trumps beauty. And the only way for the China Dolls to regain their position as the reigning Empresses of The Potluck Group is to marry billionaires. Can you say,

"Yahoo!" Oh, sorry, girls. The founders of that company were from Stanford.

It's funny how fast you can develop a taste for someone else's just desserts. Suddenly, I'm craving Jell-O, the greener the better. I'm ready for seconds and I haven't even started on my first serving.

# 10 ∘ The Three Stooges

**I am such a twit.**

How did I get so swept up in Mama's propaganda campaign that for a couple of weeks there, I actually believed I wanted to go to the Stanford University Math Camp for "mathematically talented and motivated high school students"? After getting sick of hearing me gloat, "I'm going to SUMaC," Abe pointed out that sumac is a poison plant. A cousin to poison oak and poison ivy. Well, no kidding. With a few minutes left before I head to the airport, I am itching all over with anxiety and dread.

"Come on, four weeks will go by fast," says Laura, lying on my red comforter cover that Mama insisted on buying for my birthday a couple of days ago so that I could start sleeping under good luck. So far, the comforter is a dud. After reading the fine print in the SUMaC materials, I realized that if my fifteenth birthday had been just a month later, I wouldn't have been old enough to attend.

"Yeah, they'll fly by." Janie nods her head hard so that her curls spring up and down like bungee cords. "It's not like we're going to be here anyway." Her manicured fingers run through my matted carpet. I know she's just trying to fluff me up, too. But sumac's yellow oil seeps into my head, and my brain develops a severe allergic reaction: *Let me stay! A summer of Tonic Soup isn't so bad!*

"Hawaii and basketball camp aren't exactly in the same league as SUMaC," I say. "SUMaC" spews out of my mouth the way Steve Kosanko and Mark Scranton do: worse than disgusting, repulsive, something to be squashed immediately. I flatten the wispy strands of carpet next to my hips.

Laura and Janie exchange a look.

"I saw that," I say, triumphantly, pointing an index finger at each of them, my personal Pep Team. "You know it's true."

A thump, thump, thump pounds down the hall, and Abe pokes his head into my room, spinning a basketball in one hand. Summer show-off, all he's got on his schedule is *manga* comics, basketball, computer games and packing.

"Oh, my God!" he squeals dramatically, and I hate to admit it, sounding like a baritone version of Janie. "A whole month without The Three Stooges talking to each other at least five times a day. How are Laura, Curly and Ho going to survive?"

"Don't you have some comic book to read?" I ask Abe before I slam the door on his still-smiling face. "Yuck," I say, shuddering. "Maybe math camp isn't such a nightmare compared to a summer with *him*."

"Well, you can vent all about it." Janie hands me a pink journal with giant, green polka dots on it. On the first page, she has inscribed: "Patty + (insert hunkalicious math camper's name) = Summer Fling. Nothing but the Truth by Patty Ho."

"No way!" My smile disappears into the null set when the doorbell rings, and Mama yells up the stairs, "Anne here! Time to go!"

**The only things flinging** in my summer are bodies, hurtling out of Mama's way as she barrels through the packed airport terminal like it's Sunday at a Chinese market, thronging with equally pushy shoppers. Her mission: get to the front of the line first. Who cares if it means taking out a businesswoman, harried dad and a little kid or two?

"Watch where you're going!" snarls a lady, baring teeth that have been bleached an hour too long. She rubs the thin arm that Mama nearly dislocates. Naturally, Mama pays her about as much attention as she pays her own clothes. Not a nanosecond.

"Sorry," I tell the woman, smiling apologetically at her. But she ignores me, teen Asian flotsam and jetsam in the wake of the Mama tidal wave.

"Get some manners. We aren't in China," the woman mutters before stomping off as far from the rude immigrant as she can get.

Like me, Abe hunches into himself. Disappearing is easier for him than me; he can basically hide behind my gargantuan suitcase. But you can't disguise a huge, hulking Asian elephant any more than you can me. Amazingly, Anne doesn't duck-and-hide like we do. She simply follows in Mama's footsteps, my mother who has now cut in front of an old man in a wheelchair, narrowly avoiding a collision.

"God, what did you pack?" huffs Abe.

"Stuff." I mentally inventory all the outfits and matching

shoes that Laura and Janie picked out for me to borrow and bring. Anyway, why is Abe complaining? He's been pumping iron for two years, figuring he might as well grow wider since he wasn't growing any taller. What, exactly, are those muscles for, if not to carry heavy things?

"You pack it, you carry it." Abe drops the ancient suitcase onto the dirty airport carpet. "Anne is."

Yeah, well, Anne considers a book a fashion accessory, and her beat-up, ripped backpack the must-have handbag of every season. So obviously all she needs is a tiny duffel bag.

"Hurry!" Mama yells, motioning to us impatiently. She is the angry general of our regiment gone AWOL. Punishment by embarrassment awaits the poor defectors. People turn to look at her, then us. Mortified, Abe moves away from me, suddenly riveted by the arrival and departure times at a nearby kiosk.

I struggle with the suitcase that Mama herself used when she left Taiwan seventeen years ago. Sweating, I stumble forward.

Thank God for stanchions because even Mama realizes that while she can bash through a line of people, she can't cut through metal and rope. A screaming toddler lies on the ground behind us, his hands and feet flailing, which is what Mama looks like she wants to do. She sighs heavily, jittery for having to stand still for once. Not a good sign.

Her silence is golden for all of three seconds before the barrage of last-minute instructions.

"You have airplane ticket? Registration paper?" demands Mama, staring at me like she expects me to have forgotten everything.

I nod and nod like I am a Patty Ho bobble head doll.

"Remember, Auntie Lu lives in Palo Alto. You call if need anything. You have phone number, right?"

I nod again.

Yes, I have the phone number of Mama's only sister in America. The last time I saw Auntie Lu was when I was nine. There are only two things I remember from her visit. The first is her present, dried cuttlefish that I nearly choked to death on. And the second is her fight with Mama over a man named Victor. I woke up the next morning, thinking I had dreamed about the yelling, but Auntie Lu was gone. So I'm not sure whether Auntie Lu is a stranger I happen to be related to. Or a strange relation.

Regardless, Auntie Lu is on my Do Not Call list. Just the thought of a Mama clone hovering over me for a month makes me vow never to contact her.

"You have cell phone?"

The Patty Ho bobble head nods again.

"But no call unless emergency. Too expensive."

*Save the dime, Mama.* I can already hear my summer telephone conversations with her:

Mama: You study hard?
Patty: Uh-huh.
Mama: Math camp so expensive.
Patty: Uh-huh.
Mama: You friends with nice boy?
Patty: (Silence)

And then all I hear is a click on the other line. No good-bye. No I miss you. Just a dial tone of disappointment.

○   ○   ○

It takes all of a half-second for the destructive force of nature that is Mama to blow away any semblance of customer service. The check-in lady, a friendly grandmother in a uniform, beckons us with a warm smile and one plump hand. I almost expect her to push freshly baked chocolate chip cookies on me until Mama leads the charge to the counter.

"*Aiyo,* why so slow?" demands Mama.

The smile on the old lady's face fades, sealing in any goodwill behind now-tight lips. Say hello to the unfriendly skies, not that Mama notices.

Is it any big surprise that the check-in lady shakes her head after I heave my suitcase on the scale? With some satisfaction, she tells Mama, "That'll be an extra seventy-five dollars."

Two dull circles of outrage blotch Mama's cheeks. If the check-in lady knew any better, she would have gotten on the loudspeaker to announce, "Code red. Prepare for a public display of anger." I cringe, look away and pretend that I'm with the tall, Asian guy at the next station. But he doesn't notice me. Typical.

With muscles I didn't know Mama has, she hauls the suitcase off the scale and onto the floor, and wrenches the latches open. My man-magnet outfits, Janie-chosen and Laura-approved, fling out. Sure enough, they attract attention, but not in the way any of us imagined.

"Mommy, what is that lady doing?" asks the toddler loudly, no longer crying now that he's watching Mama, the yellow Teletubby in a live performance.

That lady, I could have told the kid, is yanking out clothes without any clear plan except to put my suitcase on an immediate Slim-Fast diet.

"Ummm, excuse me, ma'am?" The check-in lady is hesitant now. She's probably afraid that Mama will karate chop her and stuff her headfirst into the rapidly thinning suitcase.

She doesn't have to worry. Mama ignores her to pick on me: "Why you pack so much?"

I reenter my reality just as my pink panties flutter to the ground. I pluck them off the carpet, and then stand there, The Statue of Lunacy with my underwear in one hand. Fortunately, Anne grabs the panties out of my paralyzed hands and crams them and whatever else she can stuff into her nearly empty duffel bag. Saved by the Geek Scout. I would say thanks, except my lips are so swollen with shame that I can't get a sound out of them.

Which is a good thing, otherwise who knows what I would have gargled out when the guy at the next station asked in startled disbelief, "Anne?"

I watch, openmouthed, as the Asian Adonis hugs Anne. He's one of the few boys my age who's actually taller than I am. Long bangs hang down into his eyes. In an unwrinkled, fitted white T-shirt and knee-length khaki shorts, he's more chic than any boy at my high school.

Mama's sex-dar is on high-alert, too. She demands, just as if Anne is her daughter, not me, "Who that?"

"This is Stu." Anne introduces us casually like we're all at a civilized English afternoon tea instead of at the airport with my luggage open for all to see. "We went to the Spring Fling together."

Strategic information so that Mama doesn't drive straight

to Mrs. Shang's house to share a cup of jasmine tea and the juicy gossip that *(aiyo!)* Anne's been hugging a boy!

I can't take my eyes off Stu, but I tell myself it's because I'm trying to decode their hug, and figure out how a hunk like him could possibly go to a dance with a nerd like her. Was it a friendly-good-to-see-you platonic kind of embrace or a friendly-I-want-to-feel-all-of-you one?

Unperturbed, Anne continues, "This is Patty. She's going to math camp, too."

"Nice to meet you," I say, shaking Stu's hand, hoping that my palm doesn't feel clammy. Inside, I'm screaming, I'm going to SUMaC! After insisting to Janie and her mom that Asian guys don't do anything for me, I am now officially eating my words as a hearty mid-morning snack.

I've almost forgotten all about my baggage claim to idiot fame until Stu brushes his bangs out of his eyes to see me better. His face is all angular *yang* with stark cheekbones and a strong nose. He asks me, "You need some more room for your stuff?"

"No, no," I manage to say, channeling confidence, poise and sophistication. An image that gets blown the second the snotty-nosed, sticky-handed toddler pokes the stuffed cups of my bra that's lying by my feet.

The truth is, I realize while my face grows hotter and Mama *hunhs* behind me, that no amount of extra room can hold all my excess baggage.

# 11 ∘ Turbulence

There are three truly awful seats on an airplane, ones to be avoided at all costs — right over the wing (if you get sucked out, the turbofan will mangle you), wedged next to a size XXXXL person (who inevitably commandeers your space), and behind a screaming child (who will throw up, if not on you then within your smelling distance).

Oh, lucky me. I am officially in plane purgatory with the bra-poking kid now barfing out his entire system in front of my seat. Not that I blame him. The plane jolts and lurches hard. My short life flashes before my almond eyes, and I grip one armrest, the other one taken by my aisle mate, Mr. Big Man on Airbus. I tug upward, as if I could personally keep the entire plane aloft in the air.

"Please fasten your seat belts," says the flight attendant as if anyone would be crazy enough to be a human Ping-Pong ball inside this plane. Her smooth voice is cut off by the pilot, who sounds like a cowboy enjoying this hell of a ride. He crows, "All righty, folks! I'm going to fly just a wee bit higher to see if we can catch some smoother air."

Yee-haw, the plane is a bucking bronco in the Not-So-OK Corral.

"Do you mind?" Anne sighs heavily, not like she's resigned to sure doom with me, but because I'm encroaching on her personal airspace.

Of course, I mind. Can't she tell that I'm focusing all my energy into keeping us alive? Obviously not, because Anne nudges my elbow away from her side, gently at first, but when I don't budge, with more force.

"It's just turbulence," says Anne, who looks annoyingly like she's not at all bothered that the plane shudders with an uncontrollable fever.

She couldn't be more wrong.

"Just turbulence" is how I feel when I think about Mark (which I try not to do). "Just turbulence" is knowing that the only Asian guy who's made my palms sweat is sitting somewhere behind us on the plane, knows I wear a bra so padded it could double as protective gear for linebackers, and has an undefined relationship with Geek Girl next to me. "Just turbulence" is catching Mama's eyes fill with tears before she barked one last order at me and then walked side-by-side with Abe away from me. "Just turbulence" is half-wanting to follow them back home.

Let's be clear. "Just turbulence" is *not* speeding toward Mother Earth's hard embrace.

I wait for Anne to whip out some fabulous fact about gravitational pull, wind drag and the expected time of impact. Instead, she asks, "Do you want a barf bag?" and reaches to the seat pocket in front of her. "You look pale."

"So?" I say, too sharply.

"O-kayyy." Anne drags out the last syllable as if it's a hoe, raking through the intractable soil of my rudeness. While I'm starting to regret snapping at her, she bends her turtle-thick neck back down to her lap and opens her book, a romance with a cover of cascading hair (his) and buffed biceps (hers).

Anne Wong, star student of Lincoln High, is engrossed in smut. Seeing Anne's nose poked in something other than a literary masterpiece is enough for me to ignore the plane's last angry bounce. Since I'm short on space with Mr. Big Man bulging into my seat, I lean over and read the words "hardened manhood" and "erect nipples." Anne's finger holds her place right above "thrust" and she lifts her eyes. "Do you mind?"

"Well, I, uh . . . You read this stuff?"

"It's just sex, Patty."

Laughter, the kind that makes you cringe because you're the butt of a joke, slaps me in the face. Anne is shaking like she's an airplane caught in turbulence. "God, you should see your face," she says, not bothering to muffle her snorts. She's so loud, the toddler in front of me peers through the gap between the seats. Anne waves at him and says, "It's research, OK?"

"Research? For what?"

Anne's hands twitch on her closed book like confiding in me is a risk. "You have to promise that you won't tell my mom or dad." She twists her body until she can study my face full-on. "Promise."

"All right, all right." Sheesh, reading a romance novel isn't a matter of national security, but I could see how it would put a damper on potluck bragging. The only literary T & A worth dropping into conversation was how at just eight, Anne read Tolstoy and Austen.

Anne breathes in like she's at the end of a diving board, and then mutters so fast her words slide into each other in their haste to get out of her mouth: "Mrs. Meyers challenged me to write a romance novel. A literary epic, for teens."

"What? Why?"

"College," she says as if I'm denser than Mrs. Shang's hard turnip cake. "I've always wanted to write one, and she thought it'd make me stand out in the applications."

I have to write a Truth Statement, and Anne gets to write True Fiction. The only Truth I see is that this sucks.

"Well . . . aren't you supposed to write what you know?" I ask.

"Well . . . how do you know that I don't know?"

The shock jock of the wild blue yonder grins just as our cowboy-pilot gets back on the speaker and drawls, "All righty, folks. I've found us some smoother air. You can unfasten your seat belts and walk about the cabin." Buckles release around me, but mine stays firmly in place, strapping me to the relative safety of my seat as my head orbits into outer space: *Could the classroom dominatrix be a bedroom one, too?*

But before I can find out, all six foot three inches of Stu are leaning against the seat in front of us. Stu, Anne's gorgeous dance date with forearms corded with muscles I didn't know boys could have. Stu, her partner in math and mashing? Hot gusts of envy buffet me. I am jealous of Anne Wong, head geek at Lincoln High, closet romance writer and object of Stu's attention.

"All righty," he says, tipping his imaginary cowboy hat. "That was interesting, folks."

What's *really* interesting is how fast Anne hides her romance novel, the core textbook for her advanced MBA program,

Master of Boobs and Asses. But as they compare notes on their last math competition, I realize just how wrong I was.

"Just turbulence" is realizing that Anne is being true to what she loves, even if it's smarmy romance. Me, I'm still searching for love.

# 12 ∘ Amber-Colored Glasses

Mama would have been tripping all over her size five feet, shoving me forward, if she had seen all the Asian boys clustered around the SUMaC sign at the San Francisco airport like it was a cattle call for every Taiwanese mother's dream game show: *Who Wants to Be the Asian Bill Gates?* I may not be able to date casually, but according to Mama, it's husband assessment time. So Mama, in her true accountant's efficiency, would have screened all these guys in less than thirty seconds apiece, and then presented me with her choice. "You marry this Good One after you go to college, get good job," she'd order, never mind that her own track record in marriage leaves a lot to be desired. The way to a man's heart is through his stomach, not ulcerating his stomach with nightly lectures.

I am waiting by myself in baggage claim. A few minutes ago, Anne dragged Stu away from the carousel with their compact luggage, drawn by an irresistible math homing instinct to the camp counselor, a man in his twenties with spiky blond porcupine hair. In his tank top and flip-flops, he looks like he should be teaching surfing instead of SUMaC, even though the group gathered around him would be more at home surfing the man-made waves of the Internet.

If I were Janie, I'd be singing, "Aloha," right about now as I boy-watched on the beach. But I'm Ho-Hum Patty Ho, watching for my behemoth baggage. It's the last suitcase spit out onto the carousel, as if it's reluctant to go to math camp, too, having already suffered the indignity of Mama's strip search. When it does finally show up, I'm tempted to hop on the conveyor belt myself and spin around in an endless loop rather than huff and puff my way to the group of math misfits.

On my way to the SUMaC circle, a petite Asian girl slips effortlessly past me with her backpack and ergonomically correct roll-on luggage. She would have been a top contender for the China Dolls Club, except her ears are pierced in at least five places and she's got a black-and-white tattoo of the yin-yang symbol on her shoulder. Even though we're indoors, she's wearing cat's-eye sunglasses.

"Heading over there, too?" she asks, slowing down and pointing to the SUMaC sign with an arm more defined than any woman's I've ever seen, including Janie's exercise-obsessed mom. She is The Asian-ator.

"Unfortunately, yes," I mutter, switching the suitcase from one gangrene-threatened hand to the other.

Her lips, shellacked a heart attack red, spread into a grin, and the girl flips back hair so long it hangs past her hips. Then it occurs to me. She's one of those Asian chicks who dyes her hair almost exactly my shade of brown, but white-balls me from her inner circle of friends. Just like the skinny girls I see on our quarterly trips to Chinatown, the ones who snicker when they see me towering over my mom and Abe.

While I'm trying and convicting her of bi-racial prejudice, she says, "Thank God, someone normal."

It's the last thing I expect her to say. I smile back at the girl; I can't help it. Making friends has never been one of my fortes, unlike Janie who collects people the way her mother collects vintage fabrics. Back in third grade when we moved in, Janie trotted over with all the kids on the block behind her like she was the Pied Piper's puny sister. "We're the same age," Janie proclaimed. "You'll be my new best friend."

"I'm Jasmine Lin. Don't laugh," the Chinese girl says, mock-frowning at her name. "Sad, but true." You couldn't get more Chinesey than Jasmine, and I can guess how she's been teased: *Hey, tea bag.*

"Sadder, but truer, I'm Patty Ho," I say, my own name striking me as funny, instead of fodder for someone else's joke. "Tea bag, meet Ho bag."

Jasmine laughs, loud and unself-conscious, nothing like Laura's ladylike titter behind her hand or Janie's soft giggle. I laugh with her.

"That's good," she says. Then, noticing the SUMaCers watching us, Jasmine blows out a low whistle, but I can't tell whether she's looking at Stu or the blond counselor, the only ones whistle-worthy. "Oh, my God, is that our TA?" I must look clueless because she clarifies, "You know, our Teaching Assistant. If that's what math does to a grad student, sign me up."

We are signed up. For four weeks. But I don't have time to remind her because Jasmine darts off for the group like she's got a math homing instinct, too. I follow more slowly, hampered not just by what I'm carrying, but by what I'm seeing. It's as if Mama's amber-colored glasses have landed on my face: "Look! There's one! And over there! And there!" Compared to the San Francisco airport, the entire Northwest is Whitesville, USA. Chinese, Japanese, Vietnamese, Cambodians, Filipino, Koreans — they are everywhere. Standing by the luggage carts. Chatting by the sliding glass doors. Waiting in the rental car lines. Speaking in Southern drawls, Brooklyn accents, Texas twangs. A teenage girl who looks mixed, like me, has her arms around a Latino guy. I can't stop gawking at her, mentally calling out her features in a biracial cheer: her eyes have a double eyelid crease (like mine!), her nose has structure (like mine!), her skin is pale (like mine!).

Jasmine slows down for yellow-struck me. "You look like you've set foot on Mars."

"I've just never seen so many Asians in one place."

"Where are you from?"

"I thought from Earth," I say, "but I'm wrong."

A moment later, Stu ambles over. For a guy as tall as he is, he moves with ninja grace. Stu to the rescue: he asks if I need some help with my luggage. I flush, but whether from exertion or embarrassment, I don't know. I'm so tongue-tied, all I can do is mumble, "No, thanks." He nods, but when his lean legs head back to Anne and her math ménage à trois, more than my hands are sore.

Jasmine shakes her head. "You are definitely not from planet Earth."

# 13 ∘ The Gates of Math Hell

Our bleached blond camp counselor cum tour guide, Brian Simmons, steers our van down Palm Drive and breaks out into what he thinks is a spooky boooo-ha-ha-haaaaa laugh. He sounds like a vampire who's become a beach bum: "Dudes, welcome to *The Gates of Hell*."

This is the math prodigy that the Second Summers in front of me are talking about? The one who supposedly is going to become a full professor by the time he's twenty-six, according to Anne, who has just whispered that bit of news to Stu? (Not that I'm eavesdropping or anything.) Now, talk about scary.

A word of advice to all future SUMaC camp counselors, tour guides and visitors of Stanford University: do not start with *The Gates of Hell*. Any feng shui master worth his hourly rate will tell you that this is not an auspicious way to begin life at Stanford.

Unfortunately, Brian doesn't subscribe to fortune-telling, only storytelling. He thumbs to our right, Museum Drive, and tells us that the largest collection of Rodin's sculpture outside Paris can be found right here on the Stanford campus. One of the signature pieces, we learn, is *The Thinker*, a guy sitting in his birthday suit with his chin in his hand. Sounds like *The Thinker* made an inadvertent trip through the other key sculpture in the collection, *The Gates of Hell* of the booo-ha-ha-haaaa sound effects. Too bad he didn't drag Mark with him.

Gosh, and here I thought hell was entering a van and listening to Anne yap about the eight problems we had to solve on the SUMaC application form. Hell is hearing everyone talk about our future problem sets like they're upcoming blockbuster movies. Spare me the exponential and logarithmic trailers, please.

So now I'm wondering, is a month at Stanford, surrounded by strange math geeks and stranger math gurus, going to be Heaven or Hell? I'm guessing the university's architects must have been just as confused about the quality of campus life because the very next stop, I kid you not, is Memorial Church, better known as MemChu.

After seeing the church plastered on nearly every piece of literature I was sent about Stanford, you would have thought I'd say, "Move on, Tour Boy." But the church glows an otherworldly sandy gold in the sun like it's lit up from within, and seeing it makes this — being here at Stanford after talking about it for weeks — cross over from surreal into real. Even Jasmine, I think, perks up for the first time since we started our tour, although it's hard to tell for sure since she's still wearing her sunglasses and hasn't spoken a single word. Unlike Anne, whose nonstop monologue about polynomial equations has put her seatmate into a permanent Stu-por. I catch Stu glancing back at me. But I shift my eyes like I'm looking out the window instead of looking him over. Anyway, he's probably checking to see if *The Gates of Hell* were left open and he's been sucked in by accident, too.

"Welcome to the Farm," says Brian, explaining that Stanford is so nicknamed because it used to be a huge farm for the founders' many horses. With all the braying in the van as we bend around Campus Drive, it's safe to say that animals still feel right at home on these grounds.

We drive past cement block dormitories, ugly despite heroic attempts to beautify them with wide-leaved plants. What was meant as temporary housing during World War II is permanent housing in the twenty-first century. As I said, the university's architects were a little hazy about the line blurring Heaven and Hell.

Brian points out the row houses down Mayfield, all the fraternities (where residents party) and co-ops (where residents cook and clean). Guess where I'd rather live? As our van climbs up a steep hill, the engine sputtering, we learn all about our future residence, Synergy. It's the vegetarian mecca of the campus. The students used to raise chickens at the original Synergy house, which was damaged beyond repair in the Loma Pietra earthquake. So we don't have chicken coop cleaning duties, thank God.

"And here is your home away from home," says Brian proudly, sweeping his arm over not to the dingy house I'm imagining, but a gorgeous mansion, built at the turn of the twentieth century. Even Jasmine lowers her sunglasses to check the place out. The front lawn alone is about twenty times the size of mine back home, and the lush grounds complete with peach and plum trees make even Janie's groomed-and-pruned garden look like an untended dirt patch.

"Hello, House of Syn," I murmur softly. Not softly enough because Anne turns around to shoot me a disapproving glance. But Stu grins at me, one eyebrow quirked up . . . in amusement or invitation? I don't know, and turn to look out the window as a flush heats my face.

Synergy looks like it's been taken straight out of *Gone with the Wind*, before the Civil War when Scarlett had enough to eat. Speaking of which, meat-eaters rejoice: we'll be taking our meals across the street at Florence Moore Hall where there's a trained chef on staff.

I make a note for my Truth Statement later: Stanford may look like a country club, but it's a school of Haves and Have Nots like any other. Still, I would be grateful to be slumming anywhere on this campus, because it means Have Not a Nagging Mother for One Month. I could be on a desert island for all I cared. That is, until I trudge behind everyone, lugging my ball-and-chain of a suitcase, into air that feels as hot and dry as the Sahara Desert. Then I realize I Have Not a Clue About Packing Properly For Math Camp.

No more than five steps into the great outdoors, and I swear, all the talk about Northern California's sublime, moderate temperature is just a bunch of Department of Tourism hooey. I am literally in Hell, sweltering in a "rare" heat wave, as Brian yells in explanation over his shoulder, leading the expedition across pavement and lawn.

Another note to self: I better start packing more lightly. If I don't, my arms will stretch even longer than they are now. I will be a mutant, the world's only gorilla-woman, whose knuckles drag on the ground. Except not as hairy. A standing ovation for my half-Asian genes. I barely have to shave my legs.

My other saving grace in being caught in this outdoor oven is that I don't need to wear deodorant. Thank you, thank you. It's so rare for Asians to have B.O. that in Japan, men can get a special dispensation from serving in the military if they smell. That's the truth.

When I step inside Synergy, I almost fall to my knees in gratitude for the cool air in the foyer. I almost fall to my knees anyway since I trip over my new pet, Baggage-saurus.

In the time it takes me to heave and haul my way into the mansion, Brian has started the tour. A bunch of kids look like they've already checked in, milling around with their parents. In front of the grand stairway, Brian tells us, "So this house was given to Stanford in hopes that it would become a mental hospital." Then his face morphs into a goofy, crazed expression, which all the kids around me copy, and I know that I've landed in a certified nuthouse.

Brian leads us to his room on the first floor.

"You need anything, anytime, day or night, bang on this door," says Brian, demonstrating for us. Jasmine looks ready to bang him, day or night, eyeing his door like it's one of the pearly gates.

Apparently, my hell is another person's heaven.

Brian points to the stairs. "Girls on the second floor. Boys on the third." Some of the boys moan in disappointment. Me, I'm breathing in relief. I've lived with Abe, and B.O. or no B.O., it's not an odor-free environment. The boys can have free run of the third floor all they want. Except for maybe Stu, who can come visit the second floor. Just as I think that, Stu's eyes collide into mine, and we both look away.

"You'll have to wait until college before you go co-ed," Brian tells everyone with a grin before taking a few steps up the stairs. "You'll find your name on the door, keys on your desks. Make yourselves at home. And the professors and I will see you after dinner, back here in the common room."

**There's a rush of** bodies up the stairs as math jocks break world records to find their rooms and crack open their books. At least, that's what I think Anne has gone to do. For a girl who couldn't leap across a single hurdle in PE, she sure is fleet-footed as she hurtles up the stairs without a backward glance at me.

I know I should be following, a good lemming who will throw myself over to polynomial equations and encryptions and whatever else we're going to study. Only I've always been a little scared of falling — falling off cliffs, falling down on skis, falling in love.

So instead, I watch the Happy Family reality show taking place in front of my face. One dad, dressed and pressed in a purple pin-striped shirt with cuff links, is heaving a trunk upstairs, a sherpa I've never had. He looks so he-man proud of himself: *Aren't I the world's most doting and devoted father?* His big-haired daughter trails behind him, a feminine echo of daughterly concern: "Oh, watch out for your back, Daddy." Even the redhead with the worst case of acne since Dylan Nguyen struts up the stairs to the boys' hall, showing his parents around, not looking the least bit embarrassed. Why would he be? His parents look normal in their color-coordinated clothes and speak so quietly I can barely hear them.

The front of the line will be reserved for me at The Gates of Hell; I'm relieved that Mama's not here to embarrass me in a thousand different ways.

Behind me, someone says, "My grandfather used to hang out at airports just to see this."

I spin around so fast, I nearly knock myself over. It's Stu. "See what?"

"Happy families."

I choke. Was my longing that obvious?

"After he moved to the states for grad school, you know, he just needed to see people who wanted to be together." Stu clears his throat, looks down at his sneakers, and then points to my suitcase. "Sure you don't need a hand?"

And this time, I tell him I do.


**"Our rooms are all** different," Stu warns me as he easily hefts my sixty-five pounds of excess baggage. He's right. We pass a condo-sized triple where three girls are squealing at each other, no doubt bonding over the syllabus. My room is an efficient rectangle. Each side has a desk at the head of a twin bed and a closet at its end. Built-in bookshelves flank the window that faces the door where I'm standing. Bad ch'i, I think automatically. All the good luck is going to rush straight from the door, through the barren middle path bi-secting the room, and out the window.

As I'm thinking this, Jasmine walks in, and gets a know-ing smile on her face, which sets Stu's face on fire. He can't drop my luggage fast enough. "I'll see you," he says.

And just like that, my good luck high-tails it out the door.

I suppose I should be counting my blessings that Jasmine is my roommate instead of Anne, but I'm trying to decide how we should choose sides. Jasmine has no such angst. She dumps her backpack on the desk on the left side of the room, the power corner, according to feng shui. It's Mama's side: her bedroom in our house, her place at the table, her sacred spot in the garden. This leaves me the bed on the right, in the creativity section of the room. I tell myself this is a good sign since I'll need every bit of creativity to rewrite my Truth Statement, not to mention finagling my way through not doing four weeks of intensive math.

Jasmine makes a big deal of examining her green sports watch. "An hour and a half, and you've made your first conquest. Not bad."

Suddenly, I am all accountant-efficiency as I open the window to let out the stale air. "I'm really not into Asian guys."

"No?" Jasmine laughs in disbelief and tosses her sunglasses on her desk. "Too bad. Me, I'm an equal opportunity dater. Black, white, brown, yellow. Except for Korean guys."

"What's wrong with Korean guys?"

"You don't want to know." Jasmine turns her back on me, putting a dead end to that conversation. "So, Stu, huh? He's hot."

"He's also seeing someone else, I think."

"You mean that girl from your high school?" Jasmine guesses and snorts. "That would be the big N-O. There is absolutely no hot-cha-cha between them. Purely platonic." She smirks, saying, "But you and Stu . . ."

. . . *are all hot-ch'i-ch'i,* I think to myself. I don't know about Stu, but my personal ch'i energy is moving and flowing toward him.

"God, you're so lucky you're hapa." Jasmine grabs an enormous cosmetics bag out of her backpack and dumps out at least a dozen blue, purple and brown eye shadows. "You can actually use this stuff." She stares into the mirror above her bureau, widening her eyes. "Not that I'm ever going to have some doctor cut my eyes just so I get your eyelids. Forget that."

"Hapa?" I don't know whether I'm being insulted or complimented.

Jasmine looks at me as if I am the first immigrant from the Land of Bizarre. "You know, half."

All I'm feeling is that I'm half-witted and a full step behind her. Jasmine must have thought so, too, because she speaks slowly like I've dropped a couple of rungs below stupid. "It's Hawaiian for someone who's half-Asian, half-white." She squints a little like she's trying to see me more clearly, but I'm still a fuzz of an idea to her. "Where are you from again?"

"Seattle. Well, actually, a city further south . . ." My mouth motors on, why I don't know, but I'm telling her where my house is in relation to the Space Needle.

"Well, that explains it," she interrupts my geography lesson.

I start to flush; now I know I'm being insulted. But then Jasmine continues, "When you visit me in LA, you'll see more white in the ads than you do people in the streets."

The next thing I know, Jasmine is unrolling a poster of a buffed out Chinese guy with the best six-pack abs I have ever seen. He's scaling a mountain cliff so sheer that my hands get clammy.

"Welcome to California," says Jasmine, shimmying behind the poster. "I hope you're good with a stapler." Grinning like she's heard a good joke, she says, "They have those where you come from, don't they?"

## 14 ∘ Kung Fu Queen

My first dinner at summer camp is a Welcome Barbecue, served up outside Synergy. The two professors are grilling the requisite hot dogs, hamburgers and garden burgers. And in the midst of this all-American cookout is an inexplicable side of sweet-and-sour pork. Only it looks nothing like any Chinese food I've ever seen. Not even when Mrs. Shang tries to whip up something other than Jell-O. The sauce, a nail-polish red, clings like glue to rice that's falling apart, white particles with a hands-off policy for their fellow rice grains.

It's like looking at a dead animal on the road; I can't stop staring at my plate even as I sit down in the open spot at Jasmine's picnic table.

Jasmine grins up at me. "Would your mom have a heart attack, too, if she saw this?"

"No, she'd push her way into the kitchen and make the cook take notes on how to make it right," I say. Everyone at the table laughs, and I smile shyly, squishing down the voice in my mind that sounds suspiciously like Mama, demanding why I have to crucify her to fit in.

Jasmine barely spares a second to chuckle with us before she turns to Brian. "Do you like good Chinese food?" she asks. Translation: *Would you like coffee or Jasmine tea after dinner tonight?*

"You bet," says Brian.

"Well, is there any really good Chinese food nearby?" Jasmine's eyes widen. Translation: *Just open your big blue eyes, Brian, and take a swig of me.*

The only other girl at our table is Katie Winthrop, Malibu Barbie. Her sherpa-father left her a parting gift that could feed an entire village in China for two years, new earrings that are blinding people on the other end of the yard. She pipes up, "Isn't Chinese food all the same?"

While I shoot Katie a veiled look of disgust, so gossamer she probably doesn't notice, Jasmine karate chops her with a comment of transparent dislike: "I suppose in the same way all white bread is the same."

Hi-yah, White Girl! Katie flushes, sweet-and-sour dork.

With a triumphant shake of her long hair, the Kung Fu Queen turns back to Brian, who has missed this great martial arts skirmish of words. Jasmine morphs back into innocent Asian gal. "There's really fabulous dim sum in Chinatown. Chef Cheng's. Have you ever been?"

"No, but I'd love to try it," says Brian.

"Great, it's a date," says Jasmine, her eyes gleaming.

Hi-yah, Counselor Boy! Jasmine's just made it to Camp One. The guy may be a couple of years older than us, he may even be a math guru. But if he is, he's got to be an idiot savant because he is pure idiot about girls.

Stu saunters into my view with Anne, bouncing a tennis ball on a racquet and dripping sweat from a squeezed-in match. He's right in time to be my dessert. If I were Jasmine, I would intercept him, ask him what the deal is with Anne, and tell him we should order in pizza later rather than eat this slop. But I'm not Jasmine. I wonder how she got to be so comfortable in her skin that she could color outside of race lines, even scribble across a bright white girl.

**After dinner in the** common room, I meet my future, and it's not a pretty schedule. Professor Drake is a slight man with hair shorn to a crew cut and mod black glasses. He clears his throat and proceeds to tell us that for the next four weeks, from Monday to Thursday, we'll be spending every beach-perfect, cloud-free morning in class. And that's not all. There's literally going to be an endless amount of homework, enough problem sets every day so that all of us will remain "challenged." While Janie is lolling around on the hot Hawaiian sand, being buried up to her neck by some cute beach boy, I will be up to my ears with numbers.

I'm waiting for a collective groan from the other thirty-four kids assembled around me, some sitting on the floor, others piled on the stained sofas and chairs. Ten of the especially advanced math prodigies are in Program II, leaving the rest of us twenty-five in Program I. For more proof that I can do math without math camp, I count eleven other girls aside from me, Jasmine, Anne and Katie of the Big Hair. (Never mind it blows my eighty-twenty rule.) On one side of Stu is his roommate, David Watanabe; Katie is perched on an armchair to Stu's right, his own golden-eyed retriever dog for the summer. The way Katie keeps leaning down to Stu, her blond hair brushing his cheek, I can guess who's got herself a bad case of Yellow Fever.

Anne, the girl who barely made a single acquaintance at Lincoln High all year, sits up front and center, surrounded by guys who are vying for her attention. Including the math celebrity, the redheaded, acne-attacked Harry, whom everyone was whispering about at dinner. He literally just won this year's gold medal at the International Mathematical Olympiad, and looks jet-lagged from flying in from some Eastern European country yesterday. Apparently, hormones are hormones, travel-weary math genius or not. He and Anne are flirting, geekzoid style, batting their equations and whispering sweet null sets to each other.

"All right, everyone, go get your homework," says Brian, dragging over a portable chalkboard. "We'll meet back here in ten minutes."

He has to be joking, right? How can we possibly have homework before camp has even officially started? When all we've done is get checked in, unpack, and be poisoned with pseudo-Chinese food?

The weird thing is, it isn't just Anne who looks like she's waited her whole life to talk about math. Thirty-three math addicts surge out of the common room. Even Jasmine, who was sitting cross-legged on the floor next to me, pops up to her feet. The one person I counted on being my fellow rebel without a math cause holds her hand down to me. "You coming?"

I tread up the stairs, legs heavy with reluctance, and remember what I did with the pre-camp homework. I shoved it with all the other camp papers into my desk at home. Out of sight, out of mind. Clearly, I was out of my mind to think this camp was a good escape plan. I've escaped from House Ho to Camp Hellhole.

Later, as I sit in the common room with my fellow campers, listening to them discuss the problem (how to break a chocolate bar into small squares with a minimum number of breaks), I realize I truly have nothing in common with anyone here at all.

I would have answered, "Duh? Zero breaks." That chocolate bar would never have had a chance to make it out of its wrapper without me devouring it.

# 15 ∘ Hapa

It's nearly one in the morning, and I can't sleep any better here than I do at home. I study the ceiling, wondering how I can franchise my brilliant new concept: Mama's Rehab program. Spend two weeks in Halfway House Ho, and you won't need drugs to feel high once you're released. Freedom from Mama will pump you up permanently, better than any drug. Anyway, it's tough to snooze with the overhead lights burning a hole in your corneas and your roommate yakking away on her fifth call since the math-attack downstairs.

Jasmine's tilting in her chair, her back to me and both feet on her desk.

"OK, ciao." Finally, Jasmine hangs up her cell phone and her chair's legs hit the ground with a smack.

Lucky her, her social life is marching forward as if SUMaC hasn't poisoned her summer fun. For the hundredth time, I wonder how she could think being *me* could possibly be enviable. Hapa is just a fancy way of saying half-breed, blended mutt, isn't it?

Jasmine is singing to herself, so completely tunelessly I

can't recognize the song. My question that's been chomping at the bit finally bolts out: "Why would you think being hapa is so great?"

Jasmine finishes her lyric, throwing her body into the last line, her head rocking, hips swaying. She's performing on some personal stage no one but she can see. For a moment, I don't think she's heard my question. She finishes her song, pauses for a moment, grinning like she's listening to a cheering crowd, and then says, "Because you hapas are so damned exotic."

Janie's house is exotic. Flamingoes are exotic. Pattypuses are just weird. Still, I try "exotic" on, but it's not a one-size-fits-all word. Now, "normal" — that's a bargain basement word I wish I could wear every day. While Jasmine's changing, I'm busy trying on adjectives: Striking, no. Beautiful, definitely no. Strange, perfect fit!

I hear a clinking sound as Jasmine throws something into her backpack. My eyes bug out when I see that she's wearing cropped, black workout pants and a tight, long-sleeved shirt, not pajamas. She heads for the door.

"We're not supposed to go out after ten," I say. As soon as my words are out, I could kick myself. Do I sound like mini-Mama, a prim and proper prude, or what?

"No, we're not," says Jasmine. And without another word, Jasmine leaves with her backpack, shutting the door so quietly I barely hear its click.

And then "we" — my white self and Asian self, my skinny self and flat self — close our eyes and fall even wider awake. How can I sleep knowing that I'm nothing but a stay-at-home tease who never strips down enough to let anyone see the real me?

# 16 ○ Truth Theorem

**S**o much for thinking I escaped lectures. Math Camp begins with one.

Why did Mama pay good money so that I could get lectured when I could have stayed at home for the same privilege and saved her a bundle?

Professor Drake, decked today in hip, red glasses, stands in front of the blackboard. Written on it: "There are ten kinds of people in the world — those who understand binary numbers and those who don't."

Spare me the math humor at nine in the morning. (One-Zero, it's a binary number. Get it? There are ten kinds of people in this camp, those who are laughing and those who aren't. Ha ha.) But the rest of the campers are cracking up like the professor is a stand-up comedian. He nods, grinning at his appreciative crowd (minus one), and then launches into an overview of the curriculum.

"Later on, we'll be studying the mathematics behind the three-by-three Rubik's Cube," Professor Drake says, lifting the red, orange, blue, green, yellow and white puzzle.

Eager faces, all bright-eyed, are glued onto him as he tells us that since this cube was unleashed onto the world in 1974, some 100,000,000 copies of it have been sold. Normal people — that is to say, people who play with it for fun — scramble up the cube and then try to return it back to its original state. But we, on the other hand, are going to use this toy to learn about Group Theory.

I'm half-tempted to raise my hand and announce that I solved the Rubik's Cube when I was seven years old. Mama was driving us on an endless road trip to the Northwest since we couldn't afford airplane tickets and she wouldn't drive on the freeways, and I was rotating the squares one way, and another way, when I noticed, oh my God!, all the colors had found their way back home. That was the one and only time Mama had actually talked herself into believing that I was a certifiable genius. Her smiles at me have never been wider. That just made her disappointment so much more acute when I walked out of the IQ test, labeled above average but nowhere in the heady realms of potluck envy.

The happy campers around me laugh, even Jasmine, who looks remarkably refreshed for someone who got less than four hours of sleep last night. I suppose if I focused on the professor with a few of my brain cells, I might be giggling at his math jokes, too. Chances are, no matter how witty I found the man, I would not be staring at him with awe the way Anne is. Drooling, I should tell her, is never particularly becoming. Still, I have a pretty good idea what the hero of Anne's romance novel is going to look like.

Slouched in his seat in the second row with his legs stretched in front of him, Stu is the math babe starring in my own romance novel. Too bad the only relationship Professor Drake wants us to have in class is one with numbers. He scans the room of math acolytes, checking to see if we are all tracking with his math puns. Hurriedly, I chuckle, too, as if I'm in on the joke when the truth is, I'm the only math joke among these math jocks.

What I loved about geometry last year was how there's no single right answer to the proofs. Any statement that ends in the theorem is right. So while twenty-three pairs of eyes are on the professor and Jasmine's are on Brian, mine return to my open notebook and my new-and-to-be-proved Truth Theorems.

## Patty Ho Truth Theorem One

*Given:* Jasmine is a Chinese-American, soon-to-be senior in high school.
*Prove:* Jasmine is like no Chinese-American girl I know.

| Statement | Reason |
|---|---|
| 1. Jasmine can kickbox white girls with a single comment. | 1. Hi-yah, Malibu Barbie. Need I write more? |
| 2. China Doll Club members giggle, look pretty, and their pointed comments only scratch. | 2. Given. Come to any one of my potluck groups. |
| 3. China Dolls do not have tattoos. And if they do, they hide them so they don't invoke parental wrath and get kicked out of the potluck group. | 3. Given. As above. |

4. Jasmine breaks all the rules — stereotypes, math camp and China Doll.

4. Given. Last night, Jasmine didn't come in until after three in the morning.

Therefore, Jasmine is different.

*Viva la difference!*

So where did Jasmine go last night and what was she doing for two hours?

    While the professor moves on to a mini-lecture on Number Theory, I turn to a fresh page and continue my own theorizing.

## Patty Ho Truth Theorem Two

*Given:* Hapas are hybrids.
*Prove:* I am a strange hybrid.

| Statement | Reason |
|---|---|
| 1. The word comes from Hawaiian slang, *hapa haole*, which translates to "half-foreigner." | 1. I looked it up. What Jasmine didn't tell me is that it used to be a derogatory term, like "chink" or "nip." How can a curse become a compliment? |
| 2. I am all-foreigner whenever I come close to the China Dolls Club. | 2. China Dolls think hapas are too white to understand Asian angst. |
| 3. I am all-foreigner when I hang with white girlfriends. | 3. White girlfriends think hapas are the result of weird, inexplicable Chinesey experiments. |
| 4. I am all-foreigner trespassing in this math camp. | 4. Given. But then again, most normal people would feel like a stranger in a strange math land here. |

| Therefore, I am a mixed-race foreigner who is a 100% mixed-up misfit wherever I am. | No comment. |

So why would anyone think being hapa is cool?

About half an hour later of scribbling furiously (twenty-four note-takers, and one note-writer), we are dispersed into five geek pods for a problem set. These are also going to be our groups for the Research Project, which we'll be working on for the next four weeks and presenting at the end of camp.

Over in the row closest to the blackboards, Anne's chest is heaving and her cheeks are rosy as she points to something on her paper. The way her boy minions are salivating, it very well may be Anne's "just sex" scene, but I'd bet it's "just math" that is getting their juices flowing.

My math potluck group includes Stu of the Burly Calves, his roommate, David Watanabe, whose razor-sharp cheekbones would make Janie go green with envy, and Ben Aguilar, with hair dyed pumpkin orange. O, lucky me, Malibu Barbie gets herself assigned to our group after pointing out that I'm the only girl in my own math harem. Let's be honest, she can't resist the magnetic force known as Stu. But even Katie is tackling the problem set like it's math manna from Heaven after a nine-month fast at the high school level. When her eyebrows lower into a scowl, I clue in that something's trespassing in my territory.

Then, my eyebrows lower, too, because I realize I haven't turned my Truth Theorem over. Stu's written: "Given: Because hapas are way cute."

I blush and bite my bottom lip. Is that a general statement

about all mixed-race kids, or a specific statement about me? I'm too embarrassed to look Stu in the eye and almost miss one of the teaching assistants strolling our way. Stu flips over to a fresh page in my notebook for me, and I whisper, "Thanks," before I put on my best studious Asian study-bug face.

It works like a feng shui charm. The assistant walks by us, nodding with approval without actually checking our work. Two and a half Asian kids hunched over a problem set = excess brain power.

Ever since fourth grade when Steve Kosanko pointed out during math that I was a weird combination, I've hated anything to do with numbers. How many different ways can you combine the genes from an Asian mom and a white dad to create an oddly tall and gangly daughter? (One.) What's the probability of getting Mama's math whiz gene? (High.) What's the probability of inheriting any of Daddy's genes? (Unknown. I've never met him, haven't heard about him, and can only guess.)

But now, studying Stu while pretending to study the theorem on my desk, I embrace all sorts of combinations and probabilities. What is the probability of Anne hooking up with that redheaded math champ who was staring at her last night like she's the Empress of Equations? What is the probability of me dating Stu? The way Katie is glaring at her paper, pressing down so hard that her pencil is on the verge of snapping in two, I'd say the probability of that white girl being jealous of hapa me is pretty good.

# 17 ∘ Model Minority

The math jailers have us so busy computing that pretty soon all we're doing is chewing and spewing math. Some more than others. Anne has thrown herself into this college lifestyle, pretending to be a full-time Stanford student, not a summer camp wannabe. She was practically in tears that the math library closes at five during the summer, wailing that she wasn't going to have enough time to complete our month-long Research Project. I could be mistaken, but think I heard Professor Drake mumble something about this being a summer camp presentation, not a dissertation.

I'm pretending to be a Stanford student in a different way. Every day after my one-on-one with a teaching assistant to review my daily problem sets, I take off on a long run, exploring the campus. I've already made a full circuit around Campus Drive, and yesterday, I checked out the Mausoleum where the Stanfords are buried. Creepy.

My foot is tapping the common room floor like it's phantom-running the Dish, the trail in the foothills behind the campus I'm planning on doing today with Jasmine. We've got a small window of opportunity before our "mandatory field trip" to the swimming pool with the rest of the campers. Thank goodness it's not some truly exciting activity, say bird-watching at the crack of dawn or something.

Time is ticking, but Brian is clicking his mechanical pencil thoughtfully like he's got all the time in the world. What's hard not to see is the disappointment in this Stanford grad student's eyes. Brian's look so clearly reminds me of Mama that I bow my head and stare at the hangnail on my thumb. My shoulders tense as I prepare for a lecture, but instead Brian asks a question, one that is worse than any lecture: "Why aren't you trying, Patty?"

I play dumb, which isn't hard after dumbing myself down since junior high. "What are you talking about?"

"Well," he says, tapping his fingers on my problem set like it's the problem, which I suppose it is. I see the obvious mistake I've made on the equation. "I just get the feeling that you're afraid of being good in math."

My reaction is second nature, honed after years of denying my math potential. Since seventh grade, I've denied that I'm good at numbers — or anything else that makes me like my math-aholic accountant of a mother. So now I say, "I'm not good in math."

The grating sound of a buzzer goes off in my head. Wrong answer, Patty. And Brian pushes away my problem set.

"You're obviously gifted in math," he says like it's a known fact. Here we go, folks. The model minority theorem. You are Asian. Hence, you work hard, you are a credit to your race, and you are a math genius. But what's the corollary for hapas? You are only half-Asian so you must be only half-good at math. Half-witted. Half-hearted. Half-assed.

"Why? Just because I've got squinty little eyes?" I ask even though I know perfectly well that I don't. The bitterness of my words startles even me, as if they've been brewing for a lifetime in Mama's Tonic Soup.

Brian actually looks offended, rearing back in his seat. "Whoa, hold on. That's like saying I'm blond so I should be a surfer airhead dude who can't add two and two, right?"

A smile sneaks onto my lips. Honestly, I can't help it. Brian considers his feet in his well-worn flip-flops and then gives me a rueful smile in return.

"What I meant was that you're as gifted in math as anyone here. Otherwise, you wouldn't have gotten in. God, your answer to the polynomial question on the application was . . ." He struggles for a word. "Elegant."

I'm so surprised, I lose the ability to build a sentence out of simple words. "Me? Math? Elegant?"

Brian nods, running a tanned hand through his bleached blond hair. He changes tactics, now the star of the buddy-ol'-pal-I'm-one-of-you show: "Look, when I was in high school, kids picked on me for being the math geek. But you're not in high school anymore, Dorothy."

Brian smiles winningly at me, but I feel like a loser. Even if I were Dorothy and followed the yellow brick road and clicked my ruby shoes three times, there *was* someplace better than home.

This mansion, for one.

The thought of returning to House Ho while Janie and Laura are still off on their adventures, the thought of being laughed at as the Summer School Dropout, of listening to Mama's endless tirades about wasting more than three thousand dollars only to get booted out of camp after a week, is less than appealing. So I promise Brian, "I'll try harder."

Ding, ding. Right answer.

Brian glows and nods his head approvingly, my loyal Toto. "Good. It's why we're here, right?"

I nod my head even if he is so wrong.

I'm here not because of any great love affair with math like Anne and half of the guys. Nor am I here because I want to pad my college applications like Jasmine and the other half of the campers. I'm here because I don't want to be up in the Pacific Northwest where it's always overcast with disappointment and showering anger.

"Incidentally," Brian calls to me as I shoot out the door, "you don't have squinty little eyes."


**I'm flooded with adrenaline** and practically sprint from the tutorial all the way up to the Dish. My feet drum an angry rhythm on the paved trail wending up the foothills. I'm so focused on their one-two beat that I barely see or smell the eucalyptus trees as I pass joggers and walkers moseying along, nothing better to do on another perfect day in Northern California.

Two miles into the run, my body is shedding sweat tears. Jasmine pants, "Yo, daddy longlegs, slow the hell down."

Honestly, I forgot about her, a couple of paces behind me since the start of the run. She might as well have been lost in the drying, knee-high grass and weeds.

Even if I want to, I can't slow down. My daddy longlegs surge ahead. The Dish, an enormous, fifteen-story-tall telescope, is just ahead of me, on top of the hill. A guard on a golf cart hums by on my right, shoots a wicked look of challenge at me and steps on the gas. I speed up, panting hard, but he's had a head start. Ten feet later, my lungs feel like they're being crushed.

*I'm doing the best I can,* I tell myself. Or am I?

Faster than I've ever sprinted, chased by every expectation I've failed to deliver on for Mrs. Meyers, Brian, my mom, I surprise myself with how much energy I have left in my reservoir. I pass the golf cart. The guard waves at me, a cheerful loser, but I don't stop to wave back at him. I reach the Dish first. So how come I feel like the sore winner?

At the top of the foothill, catching my breath as I wait for Jasmine, the irony of the whole situation sinks in. I, the giant, have been coming up short. I start laughing, and a side ache cramps me. I can't even walk, not one step. I clutch my left ribs, just under my heart. It hurts to laugh, but I can't stop.

"Who are you? Zebra-woman?" asks Jasmine, breathlessly. But her sweaty face shifts to concern when she sees me. She offers me a drink of water through the long, flexible tube connected to her Camelpak pouch, a plastic umbilical cord. But I shake my head, still breathing and gasping and giggling too hard to drink anything.

"You OK?" she asks.

Nearly tripping over a rock jars the giggles out of me. I lose my balance and only manage to right myself just as I'm about to go skidding face first down into an oak chaparral tree with peeling, sunburned bark. I kick the rock out of my way, knowing that I may be kicked out of camp if I don't get my brain in gear.

"I always thought that being short would be so great," I say. "It's not."

Jasmine looks confused. "What are you talking about?"

I tell her about Brian and how he thinks I've been short-changing myself. Unexpectedly, Jasmine bonks me on the head with her tube of water. "God, you big doofus-brain. Didn't anyone tell you?"

"Tell me what?"

"That being smart is sexy. And any guy who doesn't think so is too stupid to waste a single brain cell on . . . unless all you want to do is sleep with him. Then, you know . . ." Jasmine pulls off her ponytail holder and shakes her long mane free, "no thinking required."

"Jasmine!" I say, pushing her. "Geez Louise."

"Come on, I dare you to do this." She whips her shirt off so that she's standing in the Stanford sunshine with only her jog bra on top and yells, "Say it. Say, 'I am one hip, hot hapa mama!'"

I blush and mumble, "I am a hip, hot hapa mama."

"Pathetic." Jasmine rolls her eyes.

As I stand on top of that foothill, overlooking the red-roofed Stanford campus and Silicon Valley and San Francisco, I have no idea if Jasmine is right, but I know Brian is. I've been shortsighted. Under the Dish that scans planets and distant galaxies, I know that the world — the universe — is bigger than high school and Mark Scranton and Steve Kosanko and their edamame-bean brains. That it's bigger than Mama and math camp. That maybe I am Zebra-woman, trapped behind black-and-white bars of my own making.

I may not be able to claim loud and proud that I'm a hip, hot, hapa mama. Those are Jasmine's words, not mine.

Instead, I cup my hands around my mouth and shout down this foothill of browning grass: "I am hapa haole!" I click my blue sneakers three times for good measure.

"You're weird," pronounces Jasmine, but she doesn't look bothered.

**We ran the Dish** so fast that we've still got forty-five minutes before our "organized outing" with the rest of the campers. So we cut through White Plaza and head over to Tresidder, where we each pick up a Gatorade, having both drained Jasmine's water supply. I'm so thirsty that I chug mine before we've made it past all the grad students, the lif-ers at Stanford, clustered on the patio.

"Ready for more math?" asks Jasmine.

"Yeah," I say and mean it.

Just beyond the bookstore, a young black woman is sta-pling a flyer onto a kiosk that's papered in so many layers it looks dressed for a ragtag ball. Her pink flyer is tacked on top of old ones for parties, jobs, diet pills. I backtrack when I see "HAPA" out of the corner of my eye, and brush away leaflets until I can read the one I want.

"No way." The flyer is for The Hapa Issues Forum, an-nouncing the last meeting of the school year on "Crossing the Hapa Line." I can't believe that there's an entire organiza-tion for kids like me.

"Hate to break it to you, but you hapas are a dime a dozen here." Jasmine rips the flyer off the kiosk and hands it to me. "Proof in case you ever forget."

You hapas. I could get used to the sound of that, I think, as we head back toward the house in silence. I fold the flyer in half, holding it tightly in my hand.

A bunch of guys are playing basketball on the court in back of FloMo. My eyes are on Stu patrol, easily spying him in the middle of the court. A ball gets away from the game, and Stu chases after it as it rolls toward me and Jasmine.

"Talk about model minority. There's one coming our way," says Jasmine.

"Shh."

As if I play basketball all the time, I bend down, pick up the ball and toss it his way.

"Thanks," says Stu, smiling at me, and then he pauses. "Wanna work on the problem set tonight — after dinner?"

"Yeah, sure," I answer calmly, even though my pulse is racing like I've just run the Dish five times in a row. My eyes follow him back to the court, where he slam-dunks the basketball and shoots me a smile that says he knows that I'm watching him. And he likes it.

Jasmine nudges me. "Like I said, you hapas are so lucky."

Stu hasn't exactly asked me to a prom, but homework tonight certainly shows a lot of prom-ise. Who knew that late-night problem sets could shimmer with so many probabilities?

## 18 ∘ Equating

After swimming, showering and dining, Stu and I are finally studying in the Coffee House, or CoHo in Stanford speak. I should say, Stu is studying math, and, technically, I'm studying him. For a while, there's nothing but the sounds of people talking, plates clinking, pencils scratching and my heart thumping because Stu is sitting just a touch away.

Stu's pencil darts all over the equation we're supposed to be solving together. My XX chromosomes are getting all hot and bothered just watching Stu's XY action. Jasmine is so right. Brains + brawn = lots of yummy.

I steal a glance at Stu. He's blowing a strand of hair out of his face, all concentration.

All I can concentrate on is whether Stu really thinks I'm cute. If so, his pencil moves a lot faster than he does, because he's acting like we're just problem set buddies.

Instead of dating, we're equating.

Still, equating is threatening to one-fifteenth of the female population at SUMaC. Jasmine let it drop over dinner to Katie that Stu and I were studying tonight, and all Malibu

Barbie was able to muster was a weak verbal swipe at me: "What a perfect ho-hum first date." I just laughed and told her that I had heard worse from third graders, ho ho ho. Anyway, if Katie thinks she can fluster me, she obviously doesn't know that I'm an honors student in Mama's Insidious Insulting Academy.

A couple of scraggly guys start setting up in the corner of the CoHo, pulling out guitars and microphones.

"This isn't working out," Stu says, tapping his eraser on an errant X.

Before I think about what I'm doing, I take my pencil, reach over to his notebook and jot down the answer. He woos me with a compliment; I with a math answer? Even as I lift my pencil, I wish I could scribble out the past few seconds.

I've blown it. Kiss "girlfriend" goodbye. No matter what Jasmine says, geekiness is the wedge that drives a space between "girl" and "friend."

But Stu doesn't gawk at me like I belong to a different atmosphere. He blows out a whistle, long and loud with admiration, and looks at me like there's nothing sexier than a smart girl.

I have to remind myself, I'm not at Lincoln High. I'm hundreds of miles away, in a world where brains may not necessarily trump beauty, but at least having a brain is a variable in the dating equation.

"Girl, you know your math," Stu says loudly, and holds his hand up in the air, waiting for me to high-five him.

As soon as my hand slaps his, I know deep in my gut, where I've always felt the truth, that I am really and truly in the throes of my first bona fide case of Yellow Fever.

The way his hand lingers on mine tells me that Stu hasn't been inoculated either.

"Favorite book," he says.

My synapses are so focused on feeling his hand on top of mine that I watch his lips move and listen to his voice, but his words don't make it up to my stewing brain: *What's going on here?* He squeezes my hand and repeats, "Favorite book."

"*Possession*," I tell him even though it feels like I'm giving him a piece of my soul when I do.

"Romance."

"God, it's so much more than a romance. It won the Booker Prize." I spring to my book's defense like I'm a potluck parent, parading its accomplishments, and then stop. "Wait, you read it?"

Stu laughs at my surprise. "Well, yeah, my mom lugs it on every vacation." He has to lean toward me now that the jazz band is warming up in the corner, a lone trumpet crooning. "She said it's the travel guide to every smart woman's heart."

She's right, I think to myself. Only I've never needed a guidebook to my own heart, until possibly now. *Can my heart trust Stu?* I wonder. After all, I trusted Mark and he just about spit on my heart.

"How about you?" I ask. "Favorite book?"

I can't help it. I hold my breath, and lecture every censor in my brain, trained from years of potluck comparisons, to be open to whatever he says. Even if it's a lame *manga* comic book.

"*The Phantom Tollbooth*."

I can't keep the squeal out of my voice: "I *love* that book."

"Tock is the best," Stu says. "He marches to his own beat."

And with that, the band starts jamming, and my heart is

thumping Tock, Tock, Tock in time to a song that continues to play in my head long after we walk back to our own Digitopolis in Synergy.

None of the boys watching an action flick in the common room notices us come in together, once again demonstrating that the most difficult proofs aren't in math, but human chemistry. The girls, on the other hand, are all aquiver, noses sensing the pheromones in the air. Stu and I aren't talking, much less touching each other, when we sit down next to Jasmine. But sprawled out on a couch like Synergy is her private mansion, Katie of the Big Hair is steaming so that I swear her hair puffs up another couple of inches. Jasmine contemplates me with something approaching envy. She's no closer to bagging Brian than she was at the airport.

"Your mom called," Jasmine tells me.

I shrug; I'll call her tomorrow.

Here at SUMaC, surrounded by math geniuses and number jocks in the common room, with Jasmine on one side and Stu on my other, I get a sense of what it's like to be a Queen Bee. And there's no way I'm leaving now when I'm buzzing with something that feels like happiness.

## 19 ∘ Buildering

When I was little, I used to dream in two languages: English and Taiwanese. That ended after my fourth-grade teacher ordered Mama to stop speaking anything but English at home. In the Ho household, whatever a teacher wants, a teacher gets. So when Mr. Enoch worried about my unorthodox use of language, that was *tsai-chen* to Taiwanese. (Never mind that a year later, a little French girl who mixed up prepositions completely charmed him with her first *"monsieur."*)

Playing in my own private theater tonight is the same nightmare I always have, a Patty Ho cult classic. I wake up, drenched in sweat. My dad was chasing me with a cleaver again. Laura, Ms. Pragmatic, wonders if maybe I've watched too many *Leave It to Beaver* episodes and my subconscious wants that perfect American family; hence, the cleaver. Me, I just want to know why I can dream in color, but my nightmares are always in black-and-white. Janie says that it's because I'm more highly evolved than the average teenager, it being so film noir and everything. I think it's because I'm a visitor from Planet Demento.

"You screamed," says Jasmine, calmly.

My eyes focus on the multicolor nightmare that is my roommate. She's throwing stuff into her backpack. Every single light is on in our room, and she's even tilted my desk lamp to shine directly into my face, a spotlight of horror.

"I couldn't wake you up," she says, as if she's annoyed that I'm in bed where all good math jocks should be . . . at three in the morning.

I recheck my alarm clock on my desk to see if I've read it right. I have. But the last thing I want to do is fall back asleep, not with a knife-wielding dad on the loose. I'm glad that the end credits in my black-and-white nightmare are rolling, the details growing grayer by the second. A second feature film runs in front of my face: *Jasmine and Her Technicolor Backpack.*

"What are you doing?" I ask as she shoves some shoes into her backpack.

"*We* are going buildering."

"Builder-*what*?"

"Come on, get your hapa butt out of bed!" Jasmine laughs, pulling me out from under my blanket. "We don't have all night."

And to my surprise, my hapa butt jumps out of bed, gets into some sweats and follows her softly down the stairs.

For all the palm trees waving around like it's the balmy South Pacific, summer nights in California are cool. I shiver as I try to keep up with Jasmine, which is odd since she's usually trotting in double time to keep up with me.

## Patty Ho Truth Theorem Three

*Given:* Jasmine is a woman on a mission.

*Prove:* I am a crazy fool to be following her at three in the morning.

| Statement | Reason |
|---|---|
| 1. Jasmine is hup-two-threeing like a drill sergeant. | 1. Given. (Pant, pant, pant.) |
| 2. I am usually asleep at 3:13 a.m. | 2. Yawn. |
| 3. Only a crazy person would willingly get out of a comfortable bed to go skulking around a cold, creepy, deserted campus. | 3. Given. What was that crunch behind us? |
| Therefore, I am a complete idiot whose brain has been melted by math, so now I think it's perfectly acceptable to gallivant around in the dead of night. | Omigod, really, what was that crunch??? |

So what is Jasmine's mission, and why is she inviting me along after a week of wondering?

A skinny, feral cat darts out of the darkness in front of us and stares at us with its glittering eyes. My heart slows down. It's not a sex offender on the loose. How could it be? There isn't a soul moving in the late-night campus of hulking shadows, aside from us. Even White Plaza, the pulse of the community when the sun is up, is empty, the bookstore dark and the student union closed. Without the bikers clogging the paths and terrorizing the pedestrians, Stanford this late at night feels like a stage set.

"We can take a shortcut here," says Jasmine. We pass the Clock Tower kitty corner to the School of Education and then slip under a stone archway, no longer golden but gray-blue in the moonlight. Our footsteps echo in the long arcades of the Main Quad, where a bunch of kids in other summer programs for the gifted get to study English literature, lucky them. All the courtyards are filled with flowers bedded down for the night, their heads closed in tight buds.

"How do you know your way around so well?" I ask softly even though there's no one who could be eavesdropping.

Jasmine is silent, and then says, "An ex went here."

The way she's folded into herself, arms crossed over her chest, I wonder how recently the ex was booted out of her personal equation. Given how she's been chasing Brian like he's the last math geek in the world, I didn't think any old boy baggage had been encumbering Jasmine.

"I was fifteen, he was a senior here," she offers, as if she knows I'm grilling her in my mind.

"You're kidding." I'm fifteen and I've never so much as been on a date, much less with a college student.

Just two years older than me but infinitely boy-wiser, Jasmine laughs and shakes her long hair. "Always date up, kiddo. The guys get better."

I don't have to ask what they get better at. First, Anne and her romance novel research, and now Jasmine with her older men. I wonder if I'm the last living virgin in high school.

"How about you?" asks Jasmine.

"Oh, me?" I'm too embarrassed to admit that I'm still technically not allowed to date. That Stu is the only guy I've ever played dating tag with. That it's been three nights since our problem-solving session in the CoHo, and I have a new problem to solve: what's the next step?

"Your mom doesn't let you date, does she?" Jasmine laughs. "My parents don't either."

"But . . ."

"Don't act so surprised. You know, you don't have to do what everybody wants you to do. Good girls are way overrated."

I'm still processing this when I notice that we're standing at the side of MemChu. A couple of lights shine on the church's stone wall, casting strange shadows. I tune in just in time to hear Jasmine telling me that buildering is to buildings what rock climbing is to rocks.

"You're climbing this?" I lean back, but even arched, I can't see all the way up to the roof.

"Yeah."

I groan.

"It's perfectly safe. The route's at least forty years old," says Jasmine.

Perfectly safe is staying in bed, even if I'm haunted by recurring black-and-white nightmares. Perfectly safe is reading one of Abe's *Spiderman* comics, not pretending to be one. Perfectly safe isn't leaving Synergy at night when we've been explicitly warned to stay put after ten.

"Are you *allowed* to climb this?" I ask.

"Allowed?" Jasmine snorts. "The entire Quad is off-limits."

I can't breathe with the fur ball of fear lodged in my throat.

"Look, I can feel you stressing. Don't," says Jasmine, dropping her backpack onto the ground. "You won't be buildering tonight."

That seemed to imply that I would be climbing on another night. Given my fear of falling, I'd say this has about as much chance as Mama telling me that I'm the daughter she's always dreamed of having. So about nil.

Jasmine slides an old pamphlet, held together by staples, out of the front pocket of her backpack. A hand-drawn ice axe and piton are crossed, forming an "X" under the title, *Mountaineering: Freedom of the Quad.* She flips open to a page with a sticky note on it. Trained in reading over shoulders, I have no problem figuring out that this is a guidebook to climbing Stanford's buildings.

"Where did you get this thing?" I ask.

"eBay. Definitely worth fifty bucks." Jasmine wraps the guidebook back in a sheet of butcher paper and gently places the package in her backpack, precious cargo. "Just stand watch for me."

"Stand watch for what?"

But Spiderwoman doesn't respond. She stretches her arms overhead and places her hands on the sandstone like she's done this hundreds of times before. She probably has — every night that we've been here, and I'm guessing, with her ex, the former Stanford senior. In a few seconds, Jasmine's over my head, a shadowy ballerina dancing up the wall. Left behind on the ground, I remember that I'm cold. I hug my arms around myself, wondering what it would be like to climb farther than my eye can see.

Tentatively, I place my hands on the sandstone, feeling the rough ridges of the slabby rock under my fingertips. I hear

Jasmine's whoop and rear back guiltily from the wall. It's a hard world I don't belong to. Yet.

"You should see this!" she calls.

And I promise myself that next time, and there will be a next time, I'll be up there with her.

That is, until for the second time tonight, a bright light shines directly into my eyes.

"What are you doing?" asks a greasy-haired man in a security uniform.

## 20 ∘ Blundering

I am about to become the only fifteen-year-old in history to have a heart attack. My pulse is racing so fast it's beating speed records set by hummingbirds. Only I'm not flying anywhere. I can't hear anything above the pounding of my heart. Even so, I strain for the slightest sound of Jasmine scrabbling down the church's forbidden walls. Nothing. Thankfully, the security guard lowers the flashlight so that I'm not a blinded heart attack victim.

My eyes dart over to where Jasmine is supposed to be descending, and the man follows my gaze with his flashlight. Yes, I would be the world's worst spy. But still nothing.

He stares suspiciously at me and then drops his flashlight to Jasmine's backpack by my feet. "You thinking about defacing the church or something?"

"No!" I blurt out the first thing I can think of: "Buddha preaches peace."

That, amazingly, seems to work.

"OK, who are you? What are you doing trespassing at . . . ,"

Security Man checks his watch, "three forty-four in the morning?"

I wonder if "meditating" would be pushing it, but then every Oprah show on safety that Mama taped and forced me to watch comes bounding into my brain. Never trust men in security guard uniforms; that's rule number one. Rapists and who-knows-what kind of evil men moonlight as guards when they're really scoping out victims. Trust your instincts, that's rule number two. I size the guy up, which isn't hard to do. He looks like he's had a couple dozen Krispy Kreme donuts too many.

So I do what I always do: I run away.

The return trip to the dorm is a lot longer and lonelier by myself. I stay close to the Art Building, hugging its thick shadows as I shoot anxious glances over my shoulder. After the security guy's first warning shout, I haven't heard him since, but I still expect him to spring out of nowhere like we're in a spy movie, with me, double-oh-Ho. One big difference, James Bond wouldn't be so worried about getting caught that he nearly face-plants himself on the library steps. But I am stressed about getting caught, about Jasmine wherever she is. I wonder, does the Farm have a holding pen for students?

I skulk by Green Library, dark and desolate without any lights on. Another look around, but no overweight security guy, so I dodge in front of Meyer Library, the playground of Anne Wong and her new brain twister, Harry, since it stays open until nine at night. Anne! I groan, and add one more item on my mental list of things to do to erase this evening from Patty Ho's history of flubs. Anne cannot find out that Jasmine went buildering and I went blundering. Gossip is efficient in our potluck circle. One word from Anne to her mother and I might as well be homeward bound, both sent home and under permanent house arrest. If The Gossip Lady caught wind of this, well, let's just say that every night will be prom night for the China Dolls, who will be celebrating until they are dead.

Thanking my runs around the campus, I easily navigate past the concrete bunkers of Stern Hall and cut up along Campus Drive. Just one more sprint up a butt-burning hill, and I'm home free, not house bound. Never before has a closed door looked more welcoming than it does now. My hand is on the handle, key in the lock. I'm inside Synergy, and scaling the stairs to safety when a door on the first floor opens.

"Not so fast," says a guy.

I whirl around so quickly that I flirt with whiplash.

It's not the beefy security guard; it's beefcake Brian. He may be blond, blue-eyed and a babe, but he looks like he's channeling Mama. His eyes are narrowed and I can tell he's the guest speaker in the Mama Lecture Series.

## 21 ∘ Great Wall

Chalk it up to me verging on a nervous breakdown, but I start laughing. True, Brian's hair is half sticking up, and the other half flattened down like a porcupine who doesn't know whether he should be on the offensive or defensive. But I'm laughing so hard that I lose my grip on both the rail and reality, and slip down the last two stairs. Brian catches me, and I notice that he's looking at me like my brain has busted into a billion pieces.

He shoots a nervous glance up the stairs before steering me to his room, which makes me laugh harder because he looks like my bumbling partner in spying, double-oh-caught-in-limbo. As Janie and Laura know back home, once I get started on a good fit of laughing, I can hardly stop. Only Brian doesn't know that I'm just cracking up, the crazy kind of laughing until you pee, not the totally-whacked-out-hysterical kind.

Quietly, Brian closes his door and puts both hands on my shoulders. For half a second, I think he's going to kiss me when he leans toward my mouth, and I don't know what to do. Should I kiss him back? No, wait, what about Stu? Should I kick him? But no, the guy is sniffing my breath. Like a dog. Honestly, I'm a little weirded out until it dawns on slow-witted me that he thinks that I, Patty Ho, the girl whose craziest party antic was singing karaoke with the potluck group, am wasted. More like I've wasted my youth. Until now.

"I'm not drunk," I say, although I feel it. At least, I think I feel it. But I am drunk with the thought that Brian, the man that Jasmine's wanted to builder since she spotted him at the airport, is standing in front of me with nothing on except his boxer shorts.

"OK, so where've you been?" Brian folds his arms across his chest, looking like a dad who's caught his kid sneaking back home. That's when I'm struck with the pathetic realization that this is the closest to a father figure I've ever had in my life. "What've you been up to?"

*Correction,* I'm tempted to say, *Jasmine's the one who was* up *something tonight. I stayed on the ground.* I can't stop the giggles that spill out of my mouth.

With one eyebrow quirked up, Brian inspects me like I'm falling apart. "Look, is this camp too much for you?"

That sobers me up almost as fast as if he had just said that he was going to call Mama. Almost. "What?"

"You've never been away from home. You didn't want to be here in the first place." As if Brian notices for the first time that he's just one piece of clothing away from being naked, he turns around from me and grabs some jeans off his desk chair. While he's tugging them on, I see his pecs and think that maybe Jasmine had a point putting Brian on her tick list of men to climb. "And the camp is a lot of pressure."

Brian, Mr. All-American White Guy, has no concept of what pressure is. Stanford is Club Pre-Med with its own climbing gym of a campus and foothills and sculpture garden. My home is a pressure cooker with me locked inside. I'm trying to figure out something reasonable to say when Brian continues, "And you've probably coasted through school, so I can't blame you for not knowing how to work."

Coasted? Abe is the one who's going to go down as the Brainiac in the Ho family annals, not Incomplete Truth Statement me. I'm literally so blown away that I bump back into his side table, knocking something over.

"Sorry," I mumble and right the picture. It's of Brian and some gorgeous Chinese babe in a bikini, a woman who makes the China Dolls look like ugly stepsisters.

"You know, I'm going to have to report this," says Brian.

Funny, weeks ago, I would have welcomed this very scenario because it would have meant, bye-bye Math Camp. "Oh, you can't!" I say. "I know I wasn't supposed to go out tonight —"

"*Any* night."

"Right, any night. But sometimes I can't sleep." I bend my head down and tell as much of the truth as I can without busting Jasmine. "I had a nightmare, OK? The same one I've had since I can remember, and I couldn't breathe."

Maybe it's that Brian isn't saying anything, that he's listening without passing any judgment, but I admit for the first time, "It was my dad, chasing me, and I didn't know why, only that I had to get away. Isn't that weird since I've never met him?" I sigh, and start shivering. Now that my sweat is drying, I'm cold again. "I had to go outside."

I expect him to make a joke the way Janie would have. Or rationalize my nightmare away the way Janie's mom would have. Or give me some psychobabble the way Laura would have. Or make a sound of exasperation like Mama would have.

But Brian nods like he understands how things can haunt a person and hands a sweatshirt to me.

"Consider this a warning," he says finally. "Your final one, kiddo."

The last thing I should do now is engage Brian in conversation and possibly give him a reason to rethink his decision. Just grab this free pass from punishment and go. Yawn, tell him I'll catch him in class tomorrow. That would be the smart thing to do. The prudent thing to do.

Instead, I slip on Brian's oversized sweatshirt and ask him, "So why are you being so nice to me?"

"I'm nice to all you kids," he says, but his eyes stray over to the photograph of the China Doll. God, I hope that woman knows how lucky she is to have a guy looking at her picture with such a sweet combination of loving and longing. Brian smiles sheepishly when he catches me watching him and straddles his desk chair, propping his arms on its back. "So your dad's Chinese?"

"White," I correct him. "My mom's Taiwanese."

He looks at me like he wants to ask me something but thinks better of it. *Let it go,* I think to myself. But I'm curious. "What?"

"Was that tough for them?"

I realize that I don't know. Forever, it seems, I've sketched out scenarios for how Mama drove my father away, how she harped on him until he couldn't stand it anymore. But honestly, I have no idea what really ended them, just as I don't know what brought them together. All I know is that life in the scorched aftermath has made me parched for love.

"Mama never talks about him." And neither do I. I seldom let people into my heart, barricading them from really knowing who I am. But there's a reason for Brian's question and I can't believe that I dare to ask, "Is it tough for you guys?"

"Denise wouldn't tell her parents about me for two years."

If Janie and Laura were here, their eyes would widen in disbelief; they would screech, "No way!" But could I blame Brian's girlfriend for keeping him secret? I nod sympathetically and say, shyly, hoping that it won't offend him, "If I brought home a made-in-America souvenir, even one from Stanford, I might as well buy a lifetime pass for all my mom's lectures."

"That just about sums up what Denise thought, too."

"Do they know about you now?"

"Yeah, now they do," he says wryly. "I figured, if we're getting married, we got to come out at some point. I think I scored at least a tenth of a brownie point when I asked her dad if I could marry her. In Mandarin."

"You did?"

"It took me a good month to get the pronunciation right."

"It took me a good month to learn how to say, 'No, I'm not hungry anymore.'"

Brian breaks into a wicked laugh and we smile at each other in understanding.

"God, I could have used that during my last visit to see Denise. Talk about gorging myself," he says, puffing out his cheeks like he's gained fifteen pounds. "Every time I thought we were done with a meal, her mom came at me with something else to eat."

"That was just her way of saying she liked you," I translate for him.

Brian grins hopefully. "Yeah? Denise told me I better eat it all, otherwise I'd offend her mom."

"Definitely."

"I swear to God, I didn't think I could move for three days after I flew back home." His smile fades a little. "You know what's weird though? Being in Hawaii was the only time I felt blinding white. I mean, almost everyone I met there was Asian. You know what I mean?"

I laugh out loud, thinking about how I feel back home, an alien in my high school. "Oh, my God," I say and perch on the edge of his bed. "I know exactly what you mean."

"Really," he says. Not a question, so much as an open door, an invitation for me to tell the truth.

"Really." At last, I emerge from behind my Great Wall of Chinese Silence and tell Brian what I've locked inside myself: Steve Kosanko, being othered, Mama's no-dating mandate.

"I finally feel like I'm at home," I admit. "Weird, and at math camp."

"Sometimes you just need to expand your Set," Brian says.

"You are such a math geek."

"Takes one to know one." At that, Brian yawns and scratches the side of his face, bristly with whiskers. "OK, kiddo, I need my beauty sleep. Unlike some people, I'm not fifteen anymore." He looks meaningfully at me as he stands. "Next time you have a nightmare — or anything — just get me. Don't go outside."

As I'm slipping out his door with a "thanks," Brian pulls me into his arms and hugs me tight, the kind of hug that says welcome. Welcome in, welcome home, you are always welcome. When he lets me go, Brian hesitates and then says, "When I first saw you, I thought . . ." He shrugs like he's embarrassed. "Well, when Denise and I have kids, they'll probably look like you. The best of both worlds, that's what she always says."

I think about that as I tread lightly up the stairs. The best of both worlds. Usually, I consider myself a greater than or less than statement. My Asian-ness is greater in Twin Harbor. My hips are less than Janie's. I round the corner and pause at the bay window where the sky is growing lighter, sunlight bumping up against darkness. Who would have known that I should view my world as one big, interlocking Venn diagram, which, when you think about it, is like a mathematical version of the yin-yang sign. The real me, the one I've stashed away, is the sliver where the best of my selves — Asian, white, closet math geek, runner, friend, daughter, girl-in-lust-with-Stu — intersect.

The sleeves of Brian's sweatshirt, two sizes too big for me, fall past my fingers, and as I push them up to free my hands, I get a good look at the slash of fiery pink cutting across the sky. It dawns on me that Mama has it all wrong. There are some people — even (gasp!) men — you *can* trust without knowing them your entire life.

By the time I slip back to my room, it's almost six. Jasmine is in bed, awake and waiting for me. "Oh, my God, where were you?"

Where was I? Chased by a fat guard, hit by a laugh attack and nearly thrown out of Stanford University Math Camp, never to see the light of the campus ever again, and certainly not as a future student. All of a sudden what was so funny in Brian's room is no laughing matter. Before this moment, I had no idea how much I would have given up.

"We shouldn't have gone tonight," I say, dropping her backpack next to her bed.

"How can you say that?" Jasmine blinks. "Tonight was amazing."

Maybe for her, but not for me. I wonder if I'm allergic to adventure, because as I recount my ordeal, Jasmine alternately gasps and giggles.

"It's not funny," I tell her.

"Are you kidding?" she says and does a great imitation of an out-of-shape security guard, juggling a donut, as he chases me. I can't help laughing. My night, as Jasmine replays it, sounds like an action flick with me in the Kung Fu Queen starring role. Not the supporting one I usually play in Janie's dating adventures or Laura's environmental protesting ones.

"So where were you?" I ask, a note of suspicion in my voice.

"I hid in one of the stained glass windows."

"You did not." My eyes widen. "That's, like, two stories up."

"No kidding. God, it was small, three feet tall, max. Anyway, as soon as Fat Man was gone, I climbed down and walked around. But you were long gone." Jasmine props herself up on an elbow and spots her backpack. "Oh, good, you have it. I was worried that you didn't."

What about me? Wasn't she more worried about me than her backpack?

As if Jasmine was eavesdropping on my thoughts, she says, "I knew that you would be OK."

"How did you know that?"

"Because you're smart."

It's a vote of confidence I'm not used to hearing. I'm so drained, too tired to even put on my pajamas, that I crawl into bed with my clothes on.

"Wait a second. What are you doing wearing Brian's sweatshirt?" Jasmine demands.

"I was in his room just now, almost getting thrown out of camp, remember?"

"So . . . what else did you and Brian talk about for, what, two hours?"

But my conversation with Brian is tucked safely behind my Great Wall of Chinese Secrets, and no one, not even a buildering nutcase, is going to scale my defenses to retrieve it. For some reason, I want to keep it to myself — that Brian believed in me, Patty Ho.

"His fiancée." I tell the half-truth with a perfectly straight face. It is somewhat true.

Jasmine's questions come fast now. "What? How do you know? What does she look like?"

"She's really beautiful, Chinese, from Hawaii."

I would have thought that that would send Jasmine reeling into a new world of could-have-beens, but no. Her voice is flat. "Oh, he's one of those."

"One of what?"

"A white guy with an Asian Woman Fetish," she says. I can almost see her crossing him off her tick list. Just like that. Not because he's taken, but because of his label. "You know, those freaks who are only attracted to Asian women. Like we're exotic, sex-crazed and subservient." She snorts. "Or like we're interchangeable, every one of us, all the same."

Here's the thing: I don't know Brian's dating history, whether he's only gone out with Asian women or if he's country-hopped. What he is or isn't doesn't change how I hug Brian's words to myself. I'm the best of both worlds. And, I think, there's nothing wrong with that.

## 22 ∘ Color Theory

**W**hen I wake up, I'm not in the mood to be told anything, least of all anything about math. But it's
Monday, and it's back to math lectures and problem-solving.

The only problem my brain can handle on two-and-a-half
hours of sleep is what to eat for breakfast. Maybe spilling my
guts has emptied me out, because I'm starving. I glance at
the door, finding more pink sticky notes with messages that
Mama called and a new one that Abe wants me to call him
right away. I know I should call — at least get back to Abe —
but I head out the door instead. The last two things in the
world that I want to do right now are to listen to Abe complaining about how Mama's nagging could qualify as a new
Olympic event (welcome to my life, O Honored Son) and to
listen to Mama's billion and five questions about whether I've
met any nice Taiwanese boys and why I haven't called and if
I've seen Auntie Lu yet. Answers: no, because, and no.

So the only message I pluck off the door is the one from
Jasmine to meet her in the cafeteria. I make my solo trek

across the street to the FloMo dining room, telling myself that I'll call Mama and Abe later.

Not to be paranoid, but everyone stops talking the second I step into the cafeteria. People look at me like I'm a problem set they're trying to solve, but they're having a hard time reconciling the variables. When Anne breaks off her conversation with Harry at the über-math jock table to study me, I know she knows. What I don't know is whether she's told her mother. Acid churns in my stomach. The way the kids are gossiping about me this morning, Mrs. Shang clearly needs to brush up on her pass-the-bad-news skills.

Robotically, I microwave some oatmeal, a poor substitute for the rice porridge that I normally eat at home, pre–Tonic Soup days. As I carry my plastic tray into the dining room, I try to look as blasé as possible, as if I'm used to kids talking about me, rather than flying under the radar the way I usually do at school.

Anne sidles up to me. "What our moms don't know won't hurt them."

I almost drop my tray but tighten my grip on it, looking at Anne closely. Something is different about her.

"Your hair," I say.

Anne flushes, her hands brushing over her short hair. "I cut it off. My mom's gonna kill me."

"I like it." And I really do. It's amazing what hacking off a couple of inches does for her face. Her face with brown eye shadow and barely there lipstick. "You look great."

Then I spot Jasmine, holding court at her usual table, which doesn't include Brian. He's nowhere in sight, probably sleeping off his late-night counseling session with me. I'm relieved. I didn't want to face him now that he knows more about me than even Janie and Laura do.

My stomach tenses for what's coming next. Jasmine doesn't disappoint, announcing, "Here she is. The woman of the early morning hour."

Before I can self-combust into flames, before I can tell her to shut her mouth up — as if I were capable of doing that — the table starts clapping, like I'm some mascot of the math camp.

Stu drags out the empty chair next to him. "Have a seat, you badass."

And my badass, hapa butt parks it next to him, feeling right at home.

"Some adventure last night." His admiring look is a dead ringer for the way Mama had looked at Abe as soon as she opened his admittance package.

I catch Jasmine's eye. She grins at me, her partner in climb. Jasmine was right. Design-your-own-flavor is infinitely more tasty than being a vanilla-bland good girl. So color me cool, I smile back at Stu and toss my hair in a good imitation of Jasmine.

"Yeah," I say and shrug. If you've been chased by one security guard, you've been chased by them all.

Kids from other camps drop by our table, hoping their summers will get an infusion of fun through osmosis with the Kung Fu Queens. I know I've reached a new social strata when Katie, who has treated me like I'm less socially acceptable than a Wal-Mart-clothes-shopper, suggests that we grab dinner off-campus tonight. By the time breakfast is over, it's agreed. Our Research Project group is cutting out for some sushi.

∘　∘　∘

**Somehow, we talk Brian** into driving us to a sushi spot in downtown Palo Alto, just a few minutes off campus. After all, we need to get some Research Project planning in; so why not over dinner somewhere where we won't be interrupted? Interestingly, Jasmine invites herself along, making me wonder if she's breaking her no-lusting-after-white-guys-with-Asian-Women-Fetishes rule. With Katie practically sitting in Stu's lap in the backseat of Brian's car, I only wish that he had a no-dating-white-girls rule.

The restaurant is tucked in a quiet side street off the main drag of boutiques and bookstores. There's no sign over the door, just a *noren,* a narrow piece of blue fabric with a subtle chrysanthemum pattern. Inside, the place is about as big as a dorm room, crammed with a couple of tables, a compact sushi bar at one end and woodblock prints too small for the large, blank walls. A step up from a joint, it's an ex-pat hangout packed with Japanese businessmen. In Mama-ese, this is a good one.

The sushi chef behind the bar calls out, *"Shamasei!"*

"It's crowded," says Katie, self-consciously tucking her hair behind her ear and shuffling closer to Brian.

What she means is that it's crowded with people who look different from her. I'm so used to computing the Asian-to-white person ratio wherever I go, that I know instantly what's making Katie squirm. She's the only white girl in the restaurant.

Welcome to my life in reverse at high school.

I can't really blame Katie for feeling like raw fish out of the water in this sushi restaurant. I've always felt like an imposter when my family ate at Chinese restaurants, like the waitstaff was looking down at me for not speaking their language. A tall, stupid *gweilo,* a white ghost, I can hear them think in their heads.

The hostess looks like one of the China Dolls, all grown up. She takes tiny mincing steps toward us in her silvery pink kimono. After bowing, she starts talking in rapid Japanese, either assuming or hoping that one of us will understand. Stu smiles at the woman and says, "I'm sorry. We don't speak Japanese," but doesn't look embarrassed for not knowing the language.

Katie asks me, "What did she say?"

After years of translating Mama-ese, I can guess that the hostess wants us to stand right where we are until one of the tables leaves. But Jasmine overhears Katie's question and answers back in Idiot-ese: "As if she would know. She's Taiwanese, not Japanese. Different language."

"Oh, excuse me, Obi-Wan Kenobi," says Katie. She turns her attention to the woodblock print of Mount Fuji as if she's never seen a mountain before. I feel bad that we didn't take her to a place like Benihana, the Americanized Japanese restaurant equivalent to the Chinese Egg Foo Yung ones we make fun of at home.

"Maybe we should go somewhere else," says Katie, uncomfortably.

"Why?" asks Jasmine, all combative Warrior Woman. In Jasmine-ese, this means there ain't no way she's leaving a restaurant just because the white girl is feeling like the model minority for once.

We wait for another few minutes before a group of Japanese businessmen finish the last of their sake and leave, bowing and ogling Malibu Barbie on their way out.

"Just ignore them," I want to tell Katie, but the door closes on the businessmen and my opportunity. The hostess herds us to the table and brings us the menu, a list of sushi and sashimi typed on a plain piece of paper.

Katie won't even touch the oil-stained paper. "So classy."

My pity vanishes at her prissy act, like she's never eaten at a dive before. Like she hasn't been eating dorm food — meals made with mystery meats — for the past week.

"Isn't there anything cooked here?" Katie's plaintive voice carries to the hostess, who scurries over, dismayed that something is wrong. Change the setting and it could have been Mama rushing over to make sure her precious potluck guests are more comfortable than her own children at home. I want to slide down in my seat, ashamed to be seen with Katie. All week now, we've heard about how wealthy her neurosurgeon father is, her BMW at home, their ranch in Montana, their first-class tickets to Hawaii every February. But now her true colors come through. It's not patrician blue blood; it's redneck hick.

"There's probably tempura," offers Brian hopefully.

"Deep fried, no thanks." Katie shudders, oh so delicately, even though just this morning she stuffed her face with an all-American, deep-fried donut.

Even as Brian plays the helpful restaurant counselor for Katie, Stu catches my eye and rolls his own subtly. There's no mistaking our telepathic exchange: *Isn't this "oh-what-disgusting-things-are-the-natives-eating" just plain offensive?*

I bite my tongue, glancing at Jasmine, who I'm expecting to erupt like Mount St. Hell-Am-I-Offended any second now, but she's too busy scoping out the businessmen to notice a twit like Katie.

The hostess brings a pot of hot tea over to our table. Without thinking, I start pouring everyone a cup.

"That's so Asian woman of you," says Katie. White Girl is back in her superior element, scandalized in a pseudo-feminist way when I know for a fact she's been irritated all week that none of the guys hold the doors open for her. None of them do the "after you" thing to let her in line first.

"What's that supposed to mean?" asks Jasmine, bristling.

"If it means she's yin-yang perfect, then you're right," Stu says. He takes the teapot from me and fills the only empty cup left at the table — mine.

The fact is, Malibu Barbie over there may be blond and beautiful and act all proper, but she has nothing over an Asian woman like me who can talk her way out of getting thrown out of camp.

"Thank you," I say to Stu.

Brian winks at me just as I grin at Katie like she's paid me the greatest compliment. And I truly think she has.

## 23 ∘ Yellow Fever

"**I**'m so full," I groan as we pile out of Brian's car and head for the house.

"Me, too." Stu whispers in my ear, "I have the solution." His breath tickles my cheek, and I swear, I feel that whisper caress me inside and out. Then in full view of Katie and Jasmine, he takes my hand and pulls me down the hill, back toward the heart of the campus, calling over his shoulder to Brian, "Hey, thanks for driving."

"Remember the curfew," says Brian, shaking his head at us.

"We will," I promise.

I catch a last glimpse of the girls in the parking lot, wearing identical expressions of wish-I-were-her wistfulness. It's the way I must have looked every time Janie told me about her boyfriends. I may have wished I were her my whole life, but not tonight. Tonight I don't want to be anyone but me.

"We've got an hour," Stu tells me, squeezing my hand.

An hour. I could ask questions, try to figure out all my options, plan an escape route just in case. But I don't. I give myself up to the now, and run through the archway to the Inner Quad, just the way Mrs. Meyers told me to do.

Even though I don't know what's on the other side, I squeeze Stu's hand back.

We don't stop walking, don't start talking, until we reach the center of the Inner Quad. MemChu is in front of us, illuminated in the dark night like it's been waiting to give us a private benediction after the long, long service of my home life. I know that *The Gates of Hell* are somewhere at our back, way down past Math Corner and the Oval, past remembering, past worrying.

The moonlight is all I need to see how Stu is poring over me like I'm a piece of fine porcelain, meant to be admired, not used. How could I have written off all Asian guys in one blind, encompassing statement? How could I have ever thought that four weeks of problem sets would set back my social life permanently?

"I'm not buildering MemChu tonight," I tell Stu.

"Nah, been there, done that," he says. "I was thinking of spelunking in the steam tunnels instead." He starts laughing when my eyes widen, horrified because this is not the romancing I was imagining. "No?"

"No."

Stu takes a step closer to me. "Then that leaves us with making you a real Stanford woman."

"I thought I was one already."

"Not until you get kissed on a full moon at midnight. Stanford tradition." Stu tugs me closer and I have to tilt my head to look up at his face. "The seniors kiss the frosh, and make real men and women out of them."

The moon sitting above us is a hair less than full and a whole lot more than empty. Wind rustles the flowers that are dozing through the best part of this day, blowing my skin wide awake. I shiver even though I'm not cold, especially not with Stu's hands stroking up and down my arms.

"It's not midnight," I say, my voice coming out as a whisper. "And you're not a senior."

"Technicalities." He leans down until his lips are just a first kiss away.

"So I guess this will make me a Hapa Girl."

If there's one thing I am sure of it's this: when a boy's about to kiss a girl, the last thing he wants is to have her bust into laughter. Probably not good for the fragile male ego. Now's the worst time to laugh, but I do. Free and wild, sounding like anyone but me.

Stu doesn't look fazed, just perplexed. When a half-smile curves his full lips, I know he's never seen anyone look more completely right.

"What?" he asks.

"Being a Hapa Girl isn't half-bad."

For years, I've played the adoring audience and listened to Janie and Laura dissect kisses like they're The Three Bears: too wet, too dry, oooh — just right. When Stu hovers over my lips, making me wait and wait and wait for his kiss, all I know is that I am done playing the good girl who sits out patiently on the sidelines. I'm tired of waiting for my turn. Waiting to star in my own dreams. Waiting for my first kiss. So me, the girl who's afraid of falling, jumps headfirst. I reach up with both arms and pull Stu down to my half-open lips.

The truth is, I have no comparison set for kisses. Zero, zilch. Not even a lame under-the-mistletoe peck on the cheek. But nothing — and I mean, no books, no movies, no overheard conversations — prepares me for this lip-swelling mouthquake when his lips touch mine. Stu wraps his arms around me and pulls me so close that all I feel is his body and his lips. I whimper-sigh-moan.

"God, Patty," he whispers like he's the one who's never been kissed before.

Under that almost-full moon in the Stanford Quad, I become the heroine of my own romance. I don't know whether I'm a fake Stanford woman or a real SUMaC one, but I feel as bright as the yellow-white stars glittering above us.

It's almost ten, curfew time. We're on the brink of turning back into SUMaC students with problem sets to solve. I wonder if it's such a bad transformation, after all, as we run hand-in-hand back toward Synergy.

"So do you feel different?" Stu asks when we're just a few feet away from the door.

"Do you?" I counter.

"You're not a senior."

"Technicalities." I make a note to tell Jasmine that older isn't necessarily better.

Stu's smile is so sexy that I forget all about Jasmine and problem sets and curfews. Just as I sink against him, I see Mama.

This is no love-hazed hallucination. It's really her, sitting straight-backed in one of the chairs at the foot of the stairs inside Synergy, frowning as ferociously as the *foo* dogs that scare bad luck away from our front door at home. Brian sits beside her, hunched over and gray-faced as if all the bad luck has fled Mama's glare and is cowering in his body.

"No. Way." I rip my hands off Stu's shoulders.

"What?"

"My mother."

No sooner do we walk into Synergy than Mama demands, "Where you been?" Her disapproval is so burdensome, she can't budge out of the chair.

Our fairy-god-counselor says in a falsely cheerful tone, "Right on time. See, Mrs. Ho, I told you, nothing to worry about."

*Save your breath,* I should have told Brian. I may not be Cinderella, and it might not be midnight. But my ball is definitely over.

"Mama, what are you doing here?" I ask.

*Hunh* — she breathes out. "If you call me back, you know why." Her glare underscores her anger. "I have accounting seminar tomorrow."

Right. A seminar. I know perfectly well why she's really here: to check on me. To make sure I'm not having any fun with — heaven forbid — a white guy. Here I am with Stu, who may not be Taiwanese, but at least he's in the right ethnic group, and Mama's still nose-flaring mad. God, isn't there anything, ANYTHING that I can do that's good enough for her?

"Where you been?" she demands.

Then an idea pops into my head as if Abe has just given me a sharp, telepathic prod: *Use the SUMaC card, you idiot!*

So I become Patty Ho, gung-ho cheerleader: rah-rah-Stuboom-bah! I babble as if my life depends on it, pulling out everything I've ever learned from listening to potluck bragging: "This is Stu, he's the math captain at his high school." I even use the Anne connection, as if her friendship confers special blessings or possibly even boosts his IQ by association. "He's Anne's friend. They went to the school dance together. Remember, you met him at the airport?"

If I knew his GPA or his SAT score or what his parents did for a living, I would have tossed those to Mama, desperate peace offerings.

Unfortunately, cheering for a losing team usually doesn't result in anything except for a hoarse voice. This is true now. Mama's face doesn't soften, all stone hardness despite my effusive shower of Stu's accomplishments. I'm sure they would have allayed any normal mother's concerns about the company her daughter is keeping. But Mama is anything but normal. She stares impassively at him.

"What your last name?" she shoots at him.

"Huang," he says, holding out his hand. "It's good to see you again, Mrs. Ho."

"Huang," she repeats, ignoring his outstretched hand, but tasting his name like she can discern its vintage, or at least his lineage. Is it my imagination, or did her frown shrink a smidgen? Maybe the fact that he's got a Chinese surname is enough to placate her. But then she asks, "Where your parents from?"

My stomach sinks. I know where this is going, the Inquisition that will cover a few generations of his family. It's time to stop the conversation now before Mama probes too deep. "So, Mama," I say, "you're probably tired, and we can see each other tomorrow, right?"

But Stu, thinking he's home clear, answers, "My mom was born in America, but she and my dad are originally from Taiwan."

Mama's eyes gleam with approval at Stu. "You Taiwanese?"

"OK, I need to go to bed now —" I start to say just as Stu shakes his head. I try to step on his foot and would have lunged to cover his mouth when he corrects her, "No, Chinese."

And just like that, Stu falls into the black hole of irrecoverable disapproval.

Most people think, Chinese, Taiwanese, what's the big whoopee difference? Just ask the woman who's never taken time off work to come to one of my meets, but can march on City Hall and attend protest rallies to "Liberate Taiwan." For her, there's a world of difference between the native Taiwanese (us) and its former ruling party, the Kuomintang (Stu). Two million of (his) KMT compatriots fled from mainland China to Taiwan when they lost a power struggle with the Communists.

I wince and want to warn Stu to flee now for cover. Mama's lips thin, as she prepares to personally avenge the fifty-year-long Kuomintang-imposed martial law on Taiwan.

"Mama," I say quickly, "Stu's family moved here in the sixties. That was so long ago."

Not long enough. Her eyebrows lower half-mast, and I hear the death knell gonging on Stu. Whether anyone, however distant, in his family pulled a trigger or not, Mama holds the KMT (his people) responsible for the infamous February 28 Incident of 1947 where her grandfather along with thirty thousand Taiwanese were killed.

She says stiffly, "Not so long ago."

Of course not. Historical cruelties, family slights, less-than-perfect report cards — she remembers them all. And now she remembers what she's decided while she's been waiting for me. "You pack, we leave. Now."

"What?" I hear Stu blurt out in disbelief.

Even though I'm reeling, I have the presence of mind to shake my head at him, not another word. Who would have known that Belly-button Grandmother could be so wrong? There *is* something worse than dating a white guy. It's dating a guy named Stu.

So disobedient me, I hesitate for a second too long.

Right there, in front of Stu and Brian, within earshot of all my housemates living in Syn with me, Mama launches into the Mother of All Lectures: You Shame Family Honor.

## The Mama Lecture Series
## The Mother of All Lectures: You Shame Family Honor

Greetings and welcome to what some would say is the most controversial installment of The Mama Lecture Series. Please note that while no cell phones are allowed during this live performance, the use of earplugs is strongly advised. Due to the nature of the material, this show may be inappropriate for small children, those with weak constitutions and people who come from happy homes. For all others, sit back and survive the show.

"If potluck group know what you do here, they laugh at me!" Mama barks. "They say, 'Poor Ho Mei-Li to have such a *ho-lee-jing* daughter.'"

For the unindoctrinated, this is a bad sign that Mama

dusts off the "H" word-bomb. So now she's calling me a "wild and conniving fox," which means that Mama has moved well beyond pissed off to raging, wicked mad.

"You say," Mama begins, pitching her voice higher like a young and stupid girl, "I call you, Mama." Her eyes narrow. "I call and call and call. You not call back. Too busy" — her eyes flick over to KMT-killer Stu — "playing." She spits that last word out like it's a piece of the cilantro she hates. "I not work, work, work to make three thousand dollars for you to play."

"I've been working, too," I tell her.

Mama flings a hand up in the air, whacking away my words like so much noise pollution. *"Oh-beh-gong!"*

Doors crack open up and down the floors above at Mama's shout. My eyes drop to my sneakers. Mama is right; I'm black-white talking, not so much lying as not telling the truth. I may have been working, but not hard enough. Certainly not three thousand dollars' worth of working hard.

Mama starts another tirade. "I think, I so busy, but maybe something wrong with Patty. Maybe I take couple days off work. Go to seminar in Mountain View. Right by Patty. I think, I come over, we go out to special dinner. But you not here! You gone. I wait. Wait. No one know where you are."

Her eyes narrow accusingly first at Stu and then settle on me. How typical Mama. Make plans without consulting me, assume that I'm forever at her beck and call. And then I think of all the phone calls she made, Abe made, calls I should have answered.

Like she divines what I'm thinking, Mama demands, "How come you not call me back?"

How come? *Because all you do is yell at me.* Of course, I bite my lip to keep the truth tamped inside.

Brian, a newbie to this lecture series, breaks cardinal rule number one: never, never interrupt a Mama-logue. Mama is a combustible Chinese firecracker, seconds away from exploding. Before I can stop him, though, Brian adds fuel to her already flaming anger.

"Mrs. Ho," he says gently, "I understand that you were worried —"

However pure Brian's heart is — and I know all he's trying to do is help me — he has absolutely no clue. This temper tantrum playing out before his stunned eyes has nothing to do with maternal concern, and everything to do with me being out of Mama's control (Oooh, out a minute past ten o'clock with a boy! The horror! The horror!).

In a transformation never before seen in Western Civilization, Mama inflates into The Dragon Lady. For a woman who barely squeaks past five feet tall, it's impressive how her heaving size 32-A chest and bulging neck tendons can occupy so much space in this foyer.

The Dragon Lady points an accusing finger at Brian. "You! You supposed to watch over her."

My fellow math campers creep toward us. I can hear some of the other kids coming in from the common room. I'm sure none of them has ever witnessed such a performance in their homes where normal life includes "family meetings" to "discuss issues" and "resolve differences."

Mama doesn't disappoint her riveted audience. Her emotions are a special effects team, coloring her face first moon white and now liver red.

I feel, rather than see, Stu step closer to me. How many times have I imagined having someone big and strong come charging to my rescue? Someone like the father I never had? Now that I have my own samurai guy, I wish Stu were anywhere but here, listening to this. My entire body starts overheating as I gird myself for Mama's next onslaught, which is coming hard and fast.

"I say, you be friends with boys. Just friends." Mama snarls, "You think you know everything. Big fifteen-year-old girl. But you know nothing. You throw yourself away like cheap *ho-lee-jing* garbage."

Sweat beads on my nose. But a small part of me rebels. God, it was just a couple of kisses. What is so wrong with that?

"You make bad decision. All the time," Mama says.

*No, Mama,* I want to say. *You made the bad decision to marry the white guy, to have two kids, to move to America. Don't punish me for your bad decisions.*

I slowly raise my eyes, only to run head-on into Katie's amused smirk. Her expression is a potent cocktail of superiority and condescension. I would bet a million bucks that she just can't wait to relive this moment in blow-by-blow snide detail over the rest of math camp. Mama's chest swells, a warning sign that she's about to burn an even wider swath of public embarrassment.

"Mama," I say in a voice which sounds surprisingly cold and calm. I don't look at Mama, don't look at anyone, just my big clodding feet. "I'm going to pack now."

# 24 ∘ Lotus Shoes

Jasmine sits at her desk, hunched over a problem set. I know exactly what Mama is thinking the moment our traveling act of Blame-and-Shame steps into my dorm room: "Look at that good Chinese girl. Not like my useless daughter." Ironic, isn't it, that the girl who lost her virginity at thirteen, who sneaks out so regularly the Swiss could set their watches to all her late-night rendezvous, who tells people off in two languages, is the one I am going to be compared to for the rest of my life as the Shining Example of Obedience. Unlike me, The Waster of Good Opportunities, not to mention three thousand bucks.

Then Mama breathes out, *hunh!* I look around, queasy, wondering what in this small room could possibly make Mama hiss like a pissed-off Komodo dragon. I spot the culprit. Heaven forbid, it's the glossy poster of the shirtless rock-climbing wonder. Damn it, why did we staple Mr. Hot Chinese Climber Guy on *my* side of the room? Mama's cheeks flush. She climbs onto my bed. With one swift pull, she rips him and all hints of sexual temptation off the wall, leaving only the poster's corners clinging for safety. Goodbye, Asian hottie. Hello, Asian hothead.

"You pack," the hothead orders.

I half-expect Jasmine to say something about her shredded poster, but she looks between me and Mama, adding it up. It's a simple equation:

One half-mad Asian mother + one silent half-Asian daughter = One Highly Combustible Situation.

I stand still as a Rodin statue, too shocked to do anything other than watch Mama grab clothes out of my closet and fling them into my suitcase. Somehow, my stuff has expanded in the brief week of freedom. Not everything fits back inside Mama's old suitcase. Coming to, I scoot over to heave myself on top of the wide-mouthed luggage.

"I'll take care of it," Jasmine murmurs, shooting me a sympathetic look when my frantic wrestling match with the suitcase leaves me no closer to closing the two-inch gap. Mama is *hunh*-ing all the while in the background.

I nod, leaving Brian's sweatshirt and a few random shirts and shorts on my bed. Just as I latch the suitcase, I swear I can hear *The Gates of Hell* creaking open and sucking me back into Hellhole Ho.


When Mama is at the wheel, the highway patrol would be doing a great public service by issuing an all-points bulletin for everyone to stay off the road. Tonight, Mama's driving is more erratic than normal. Not that my driving tonight would have been any better. My fists are clenched in my lap as I glare out the window. Wouldn't you know it? I didn't even want to come to this stupid camp in the first place, but now that I want to stay, Mama whisks me away.

I should have predicted this because, heaven forbid, I was having fun.

I was actually feeling free for the first time in my caged-up, cramped-in and controlled life.

I actually had a boyfriend — or at least a guy who thought I was seriously cute. Not to mention interesting, smart and sexy.

But oh, no, with Mama's sex-dar perpetually on high alert, we'll have none of *that*. My life, or the way Mama wants me to live it, is supposed to be miserable, isolated and under her thumb.

"Not all guys are bad, Mama," I mutter, keeping my eyes out the window and off her face.

"You wrong!" she snaps. "You know nothing. I tell you, need know boy long time before know if he a Good One."

How long? I don't want to live on guard all the time, with foo dogs stationed around my heart, waiting for a guy to mess up so that I can scare him out of my life. Like Mama did with my father.

"You think can trust everything people tell you. You just like my new client. He think he so smart because he a doctor. He tell me, Yes, turned in all receipts, Mrs. Ho. Yes, everything in order. But I say, where is twenty-five thousand dollars? Not in bank. He say, Oh, Mrs. Ho, you make a mistake." *Hunh!* Mama slaps the steering wheel with her open hand. "Office manager took! He think can trust her. She so nice, so pretty. Work for him two years." Mama's voice deepens into a facsimile of the doctor's, if he lost his grasp on verb tenses: "I can't believe she steal from me!"

This tirade ends with an especially loud, satisfied, told-you-so *hunh!*

For no apparent reason, Mama slams on the brakes in the middle of a barely lit street. I bite down on my tongue, drawing blood. I muffle my moan, not wanting to draw Mama's attention back to me. The car behind us screeches to a stop, nearly rear-ending us. I can only hope it's not a cop. If it is, I'll have to explain that Mama hasn't been drunk driving, unless you count her boozing big time on my sins. Yes, Officer, I kissed a boy; so throw away the lock and key. Come to think of it, being imprisoned in House Ho might be a blessing since I can't face all the SUMaCers who've witnessed my mom, a grown woman, have an all-out, mental meltdown.

Five lurches and eight slammed brakes later, we finally park in front of Auntie Lu's home, a small gingerbread cottage. The only thing missing from this fairy tale setting is the wicked witch who happens to be sitting next to me. Mama glowers like she plans to toss me into a black cauldron and clang the lid right on top of my empty head. Tonic Soup with a dash of Disobedient Daughter. A special Chinese delicacy.

The front door swings open, and a younger version of Mama bustles out with a delighted smile. All looks of happiness fade when Auntie Lu sees me. Her brows furrow into the same worried expression Mama wears 24/7. I seem to have that effect on first-generation women tonight.

"Victor still not here, right?" Mama demands, forgetting to speak in Taiwanese.

Auntie Lu's mouth tightens for a split second, the way Mama's does when she's displeased about something. "I told you, he's on business for another two weeks."

And then it occurs to me, Mama's random drop-in visit

may not have been entirely to spy on me or to attend a seminar on how to maximize the new version of her accounting software, but to take advantage of the infamous Victor being out of town. If I were Auntie Lu, I'd tell my mom to get over herself. I mean, who Auntie Lu — a grown woman — is living with shouldn't be any concern of Mama's, but Auntie Lu's lips relax back into a smile.

"*Lai! Chia bung,*" says Auntie Lu.

Who can think of eating at a time like this? Obviously, these women can. Auntie Lu takes Mama's black briefcase from her and holds Mama's arm, leading her like she's an old lady, an *obasan.* In the shadowed driveway, Mama really does look like one of those humpbacked old women who haunt Chinatown with their plastic bags and shuffle-step walks. My throat tightens, and I wade through Mama's trail of disappointment, my back bending from my suitcase and hers.

By the time I make it inside, Mama and Auntie Lu have disappeared somewhere in the house. Mama's practical slip-on flats, soles barely there, are lined next to Auntie Lu's red-beaded, dainty mules.

Left on my own, I shed my sneakers in the far corner, outcasts like me. Then I stand there awkwardly, barefooted on the cool tile floor, not sure what I should do when Auntie Lu walks out of the kitchen toward me. Her hot pink slippers barely make a sound. I gird myself for another lecture, but instead Auntie Lu hugs me, tight, hard and quick.

"You can sleep in my office tonight," she says. "First door on the right. Why don't you put your mama's luggage in the guest room, across from my room?" She casts a look toward the kitchen and murmurs, "We'll sort this all out."

Then Auntie Lu disappears back into the kitchen, where I

can smell Mama's dinner, cooling there for the past three hours while she simmered in Synergy. From the sounds of it, Mama is having a grand old time talking about me. Her sister-talk is all big-worded Taiwanese that I don't understand, except for my angry-staccato name as I walk quickly past with Mama's luggage and briefcase.

I know then that I can't go home with Mama. I don't want to hear her harping on me the whole summer, not when I'll have her undivided, nagging-you-not-good-enough attention all to myself once Abe abandons me for college. I'll do anything to stay at camp — if I only knew how.

As I place Mama's things inside the guest room, my gaze falls on the laughing Buddha on top of the bookshelf. I bunch my fists at my side so I don't give in to my impulse to pull him off and smash him onto the ground. If I didn't have to face the Wrath of Mama, part two, I'd do it. I glare at Buddha. There is nothing joyful about being me right now, I want to tell him. This is no laughing matter, not when you've got a crazed, irrational mother who doesn't realize that we live in twenty-first-century America, not the Taiwan of her girlhood.

My stomach cramps as I imagine Mama conspiring with Auntie Lu in the privacy of the kitchen. I'm sure first thing tomorrow, we'll be on a plane, heading back up to Washington. My life here is already ruined; I've been publicly sliced and diced with Mama's cleaver-sharp tongue. Stu has got to think that I'm a nutcase, and if he doesn't, Katie is sure to make me out to be the strangest Chinesey experiment ever to go wrong.

When I head downstairs to grab my luggage, I hear my name followed by "ho-lee-jing" and "boy." Self-preservation prompts me to bunker down in Auntie Lu's living room, where I can listen to what Mama's planning to do with me.

Most arsty-fartsy living rooms I've been in, like the ones Janie's mother designs or the ones Janie ogles in magazines, are hardly meant for living. They're color-coordinated salons of style designed for pleasing the eye rather than the butt. But Auntie Lu's is a clashing, mismatched, multicultural community center. Oil paintings done in the Old Masters style hang next to modern, bright acrylics. An overstuffed, red velvet sofa is parked on top of a striped kilim rug. Behind it is a display of African masks and a line of jade green ceramic pots.

The painting above the fireplace makes me jerk away uncomfortably — a young Chinese girl in a traditional cheongsam dress whose legs end in pinpoints and whose mouth is bound. I can't get the image out of my head no matter where else I look, so I step up close to it. The creepy part is that the girl looks perfectly placid like she hasn't even noticed that she's gagged. I touch my own mouth that's been covered with Stu kisses one moment and bitten the next to keep myself from railing back at Mama.

At the bottom corner of the painting, I spot the artist's signature: Louise Ho next to a red chop, her Taiwanese name. I had no idea Auntie Lu was an artist, but then again, I don't know much about her except that she's been a missing person in my life. Just like my dad, another victim of Mama's haranguing. Oddly, I can hear Mama and Auntie Lu, still chatting away like long-lost best friends. Nothing reunites people more than someone else's scandal.

Two scrolls with Chinese calligraphy flank the French doors. Peering outside, I can barely make out the shadowy outline of a few sculptures in the tiny garden outside. Finally, I'm drawn to the back wall, entirely covered with eight-by-ten,

black-and-white photographs of people of all ages and eth-
nicities, smiling, grinning, laughing. It's an openmouthed
and closed lipped montage of joy. The white mats are signed
by the same man: Victor Jackson, Auntie Lu's mystery man.

The kitchen is finally silent. I hold my breath as the sisters
plod along the hall, but they don't stop to lecture me in
stereo. They head straight up the stairs. And soon, a door
closes quietly behind them, locking me out.

I pluck a couple of dead, brown leaves off the bamboo
squatting in a green ceramic pot to the side of the fireplace.
Then I collapse onto the red sofa and pick up one of the art
books heaped on the leather ottoman. The weird Dali paintings feel too close to my mixed-up mental state, so I put the
coffee table book back down. Just then, a door upstairs opens
and the low undertone of the sisters' conversation seeps out.
To clue into my fate I tiptoe to the Japanese *tansu* chest in the
hall. The chest looks like a miniature staircase that leads to
nowhere, with each successive layer shorter than the one below it. On every step is a different pair of shoes the size of my
palm, all framed in matching shadow boxes. Some have tiny
wedge-shaped heels. Others are flat. All are embroidered, yel-
lowing with age and fraying on the bottom. I can't take my
eyes off of the pair stitched with purple blossoms, recognizing
the shoes though I've never seen anything like them before.

"These were your great-great-grandmother's," murmurs
Auntie Lu.

I rear back guiltily from the *tansu* as Auntie Lu glides
down the staircase. She shoots me a glance that I can't read,
before reaching for the shadow box with the shoes I had
been studying. She holds them up to the spotlight and says,
"Lotus shoes."

"They look like doll shoes." China Doll shoes, I think to myself. Way too small for me or any normal human being for that matter.

"Dolls who had their feet broken and bound so that they wouldn't grow bigger than three or four inches long. Like lotus flowers."

I grimace, curling my toes in imagined pain. "Why?"

Auntie Lu snorts. "Some scholars say that women bound their feet to get a sexy walk kind of like the way women wear four-inch heels today."

I think about life with Mama where I've never even gotten the Sex Talk, where no makeup is permitted and, certainly, no dating Stu is allowed. Somehow, thousands of years of foot-binding to obtain a sexy walk just doesn't compute. Unconsciously, I glance over at Auntie Lu's gagged girl over the fireplace.

"It was to keep girls from getting into trouble, right?" I ask. Chastity belts for feet. If you can't walk, you're not likely to sneak out in the middle of the night, say to kiss a secret lover in the Quad or climb up the side of a building.

Auntie Lu shrugs and holds up one hand, bending her fingers under her palm. "Imagine hobbling on top of your toes like that every day, starting when you were five."

What a way to imprison women: cripple them so they can't run away. "Hell on heels," I mumble.

"That's very clever." Auntie Lu laughs, nodding and looking at me over the lotus shoes. "We are so lucky, aren't we?"

We. Not "you." Which is the way Mama would have put it: *you* so lucky. Making it sound like my being lucky is a bad thing. But the way Auntie Lu says it, we're a team, lucky together. Except tonight is proof that I'm anything but lucky.

Who can understand why Mama does half the things she does? She never explains. Her reasons are hidden away like twisted feet tucked in gorgeous, handmade shoes.

"She thinks you're throwing away your perfect chance for a good future," says Auntie Lu gently. "You know, your mama turned down a fellowship at the University of Taipei in math to run off with your father."

"She did?"

Auntie Lu nods and shoots a cautious glance up the stairs. Mama's door is still closed. What I've just learned is more than anyone's shared with me about Mama's past — *my* history. I have hundreds more questions, but Auntie Lu's lips are pursed, looking uncannily like Mama when she locks in her thoughts. So I'm surprised when Auntie Lu steps closer to me and whispers like the words are hard to say, harder to hear, "And then when things didn't work out, she regretted her decision . . ."

Her voice trails off, but not before I follow that thought down the path of Mama's life. How Mama regretted marrying her white guy, having children. Having me. From somewhere in the past, I remember overhearing Mama tell the potluck group: "Life lot easier with no children."

"Out of all of us, our parents said that Mei-Li was the one who would do something great, be someone. A research scientist, an engineer," murmurs Auntie Lu. She gently dusts off one of the shadow boxes on the *tansu*. "Professor Ho."

Guess what? Mama lectures me enough to qualify as a college professor. As soon as that thought pops into my head, I'm ashamed and try to blot it out by blurting aloud: "Your English is so good!"

For the second time in a minute, I'm horrified at myself. I

hate it when the old fogies back at home look astonished that I don't speak with an accent. One time at the grocery store, a fat grandma type at the register said, "Why, I barely detect any Chinese in your words." Funny, I wanted to snap back at her, I detect a lot of ignorance in yours.

But Auntie Lu looks pleased instead of offended. "Thank you," she says and blows a piece of lint off the shadow box in her hands. "Your mother didn't have the luxury of studying English the way I got to. She was too busy taking care of you and Abe. And working. Always working. I'm not sure how she found the time to study for her CPA."

Auntie Lu opens the box where the tiny purple shoes are pinned onto a piece of taupe suede, specimens from a society that seems so far removed from me.

"Your great-great-grandmother was one tough lady. Once when she must have been about ninety years old, she rode the train by herself to our house in Taipei. Step, step, step, she walked until she made it to our front door. She kept pointing to these shoes." Auntie Lu frees the lotus shoes from the shadow box and traces the delicate, purple embroidery. "Plum blossoms, see? They bloom even in adversity."

Gently, Auntie Lu unfurls my fist to nest the shoes in my open palm, the delicate shoes almost weightless. "Even in the middle of the winter with snow on their branches, they bloom."

# 25 ∘ Walking Tall

I'm bedded down for the night on the musty-smelling, pull-out couch in Auntie Lu's office. It's not like I need to be well rested for tomorrow's flight back home. In fact, it'll be a godsend if I'm so tired that I fall asleep next to Mama on the plane so I don't have to feel her disappointment pricking me. The sound of the sisters gossiping in the living room, catching up on which cousins back in Taiwan have gotten married, divorced and fat, is like the pattering of rain at home. Talk, talk, talk, laugh. Talk, talk, talk, *aiyo!*

I throw off the covers, drowning in the downpour of my thoughts. All I know is, I have to stay at math camp. I barely take three steps from the sofa bed, and my hip bumps into Auntie Lu's desk, an enormous antique Chinese scholar's table. Holding my bruised hip, I pace toward the door, and trip on a stack of books on the floor. I suppose most people would find Auntie Lu's home office comfortable. But let me be the first to say, this room is a living feng shui hell. How can I think of a way out of my own mess when I can't even walk through Auntie Lu's?

I hop up and down, holding my throbbing big toe, and wiggle it gingerly before I put my weight back on it. I limp to the bed and groan, as unladylike a sound as you can make. And I realize, I am no little lady who has to wait for her fate.

Before I chicken out, I creep down the stairs and see the sisters on the couch, their heads bowed close together as one nods and the other speaks. I'm trembling so badly that I place a hand on the *tansu* chest to steady myself. If I thought running into a security guard was scary, it's nothing compared to confronting Mama. I brush the hair out of my face and tuck the stray strands behind my ears. Seriously, I doubt I can do it, talk to Mama. *Coward,* I yell at myself even as I turn back up the stairs. And then, I see the lotus shoes, the ones with the plum blossoms, glowing silvery-purple under the special lights mounted over the *tansu.*

Plum blossoms blooming right now in adversity.

My big toe still hurts. I hobble toward the living room, unable to fathom how my great-great-grandmother with her two crippled feet could have walked anywhere, much less a couple miles from the train station to Mama's old home. *Step, step, step.*

I look down at my big feet that are three times the size of hers. My big feet that could crush any China Doll shoe.

My big feet that aren't maimed or bound.

"I really want to go back to math camp," I announce as soon as I step inside the living room. Now that I'm saying my speech aloud, I realize I have a better chance of acing my still-to-be-worked-on Truth Statement than convincing Mama to let me stay.

Mama's eyebrows are stitched together in a perma-frown. She's back to doing her foo dog impression, only I'm the one she's trying to scare away.

"You just want have *fun*," Mama says, her lips twisting at the "F" word.

What's wrong with having fun? My irritation ignites like dry grass, but I catch Auntie Lu looking steadily at me like she's reminding me to stay with my rational, logical speech instead of engaging in this endless loop of accusation.

Quietly, I say, "Mama, I've always brought home great report cards. You can trust me."

"You not trust me," counters Mama, sitting up tall and straight. "I tell you, best thing is you go to good college. Get good job. Take care of self. Then find Good One and marry."

This is not going the way I had rehearsed upstairs in Auntie Lu's office, but I grasp onto Mama's flowchart for my life. "I'm trying to get into a good college. Last year, a third of the math campers got into Stanford."

Studying Mama the way meteorologists must scrutinize the slightest change in winds and clouds to predict storms, I notice the lines around her mouth relax almost imperceptibly.

"And you've already paid for camp. There are no refunds," I say, inching closer to the sisters on the couch. "It would be a waste of three thousand dollars if I don't finish."

*Hunh.* I hear it, a faint sound bordering on thoughtful. Before it can build to Mama's normal battle cry, I speed through the last part of my speech: "What if I stayed here with Auntie Lu for the rest of camp? I can walk to school, and I can get a job and pay Auntie Lu." I can't help the pleading, wheedling tone in my voice when Mama's face remains stoic: "Or Auntie Lu, I can help you out around the house if you want."

Usually, at home, I welcome this rare, wordless respite of Mama's silence. It's one less chance of some criticism flinging out of her mouth. Funny, now that she's playing the In-scrutable Asian, all I want to do is shake her: *Say something!*

Saved by Auntie Lu, who beams and claps like my idea is a true gift, not a ploy to stay at camp. "That's a *wonderful* idea, Patty." She turns to Mama. "Mei-Li, she's right. It would be a waste if she didn't finish camp. And I'll watch over her. She can help me organize things. You were just saying I needed to space-clear."

I doubt that Mama put it in those polite, politically correct terms. She probably said something like; "Your house is dis-grace! Bad luck everywhere! No wonder no husband. No children."

I hate to admit it, but I agree. If Auntie Lu's office is any in-dication, her entire home needs desperate and immediate space-clearing.

Mama's lips remain squeezed tight, and I resign myself to the rest of the summer enduring Abe's teasing that I couldn't hack it for a week on my own. My stomach lurches. Oh, God, and there are the gloating China Dolls to face down. But then, miracle of miracles, Mama says to me, "You work hard."

I nearly trip over my feet, I'm so stunned.

I, Patty Ho, have scored the first-ever victory for myself in Ho family history.

"You not make me worry." And then Mama bites her lip the way I do when I'm uncertain. Or when I want to check my emotions into the coatroom of my heart. "You call me."

"I will," I promise.

Maybe it's the contrast of Mama's tense face against the portraits of happy people behind her back. Suddenly, I can imagine how worried she must have been since she hadn't heard from me. After all those articles she's clipped for me since I was eight or nine, the ones about the missing kids, the raped girls, the teens who were left for dead, I should have known what kind of nightmares were keeping her up at night. Just like mine. If I had been a good girl — or at least a considerate one — I would have returned Mama's phone calls right away. Two minutes of my time and Mama wouldn't have felt like she had to fly out to check up on me.

"Go to class. Do homework," Mama continues, listing her terms and conditions. What shocks me now is the slightest of smiles that creases Mama's lips, like she thinks she's the victor. "You stay."

# 26 ∘ The Return of the Kung Fu Queen

First thing the next morning, we drop Mama off at her seminar in Mountain View, about fifteen minutes from Auntie Lu's home. Tall men in crisp shirts and women in heels are descending on the Intuit headquarters, as eager for the training seminar on the new software product as my math camp buddies are for problem sets. Mama looks so fragile clutching her briefcase half the size of her body that I want to go in with her, carry some of her burden.

"Don't worry about your mama," says Auntie Lu, giving me a quick smile. "She'll set them straight about who's the boss in five minutes."

"You mean, two minutes." I grin back at Auntie as I scoot into the front seat, taking Mama's place.

But when Auntie Lu pulls into the parking lot at Stanford, she looks surprised that I'm not bounding out of her mini-Cooper, all eager excitement to be back at math camp. The car is idling, and so is my butt. It's not exactly as if my daddy longlegs can't unfurl themselves out her matchbox-sized car (although I have had more comfortable rides, say on a unicycle circa sixth grade, PE class). Pure dread and nervous perspiration glue me to the leather seat.

"Everybody has been embarrassed by their mom at one point or another," says Auntie Lu, encouragingly.

My eyebrows jump so high, I become a plastic surgeon's poster girl for face-lifts. Embarrassing is watching Mama bargain with a salesperson as if we were in some outdoor market in Hong Kong, not in a clothing store in Seattle. All-out public humiliation is getting tongue-lashed in front of everyone at SUMaC, including my first would-be boyfriend.

"Not everyone has been yanked out of summer camp by their mother."

Auntie Lu just shrugs. "Who cares what people think? In art, a little controversy is always a good thing." She brushes the bangs out of my face and taps my hand that's gripping my knee. "Coming back is what you want, isn't it?"

It is. The last thing Mrs. Meyers said to me at the end of the year about running through doors echoes in my ears so loudly, she could have been squeezed into this car with us. I square my shoulders, at least as much as I can while wedged into this bento box of a car, and open the door wide.

"Thanks for the ride," I tell Auntie Lu as I wriggle out.

"*Aiyo,* Patty!" For a second, she sounds unnervingly like my mother. I lean back in the car just in time to see Auntie Lu's smile plummet into a frown. She wails, "Your shirt is soaking wet! You can't have a triumphant return looking like *that.*"

The T-shirt I borrowed from Janie for the camp clings to my back. I reach behind, thinking I could air it dry, but the cotton is drenched through on my back and, glancing down, under my arms. Auntie Lu does have a point there. It's one thing to towel sweat off your forehead and another to look like a saturated towelette.

Auntie Lu digs in the backseat where she stashed extra yoga clothes. "A-ha!" she cries victoriously, and waves an orange tank top with a keyhole opening in the front. "Change into this."

"I can't wear that! You're like five sizes smaller than me."

"Come on, just put it on. No one will see you, it's so early."

Years of surreptitious surveillance to make sure no one is in the near vicinity when I step out with perennially mismatched Mama works to my advantage now. I do a swift, expert 360 scan through the windshield and rearview window. Auntie Lu's right, not a soul in sight. Not in the street behind us. Not on the pathway to our side. So I whip off my damp T-shirt, toss it onto the floor and slip into her baby-sized tank. As I get out of the car, I groan. The tank top is skimpier than anything I've ever worn. Worse, it rides up my midriff, a couple of inches over my belly button. Mama would have had a coronary at my exposing so much skin, but Auntie Lu says, "You look hot."

Before I can ask if she has anything else in the backseat, a chorus of "Patty!" rings out. Then I hear a familiar condescending snicker, "Get some clothes on, Ho."

Katie of the Big Hair is leading a marching band of SUMaCers toward Math Corner. Miss Manners-in-Training looks positively scandalized that anyone could be wearing an itty bitty top the size of a bra. Let's get real, from my side view, I could pass as a preadolescent boy, which Abe constantly points out to flat as a pattycake me. So I'm not sure what the Big Deal is, when it's obviously not my boobs.

It's a binary decision: either I can melt into a sweat puddle of embarrassment or I can pretend that I don't care that I'm half-naked. The latter is more palatable. I've already eaten my fill of shame. So I shimmy my shoulders and hips like I'm my very own welcome home banner.

Jasmine hoots, "Woo hoo!"

I stop my futile yank-and-tug when Stu eyes my abs like he's spotted nirvana.

"Now, *that's* a triumphant return," says Auntie Lu approvingly and drives off. I stare after her cherry red car in wonder. Is attitude truly the only thing separating embarrassment from triumph? That a little sass could turn you from a social zero to social hero?

There's got to be something to that, I think, when I run over to join the group, screaming, "I'm back!" Stu wraps his big, strong, trustable arms around me. And when I peek over his shoulder to smile at Jasmine, I notice that Katie looks deflated, a cream puff without her fluff. *Hi-yah, White Girl! The Kung Fu Queen is back in town.*

"My turn," Jasmine tells Stu and throws her arm around me like we're the inaugural members of the Kung Fu Kick-Ass Club. I never thought I'd be happy to see Building 380 or look forward to three straight hours of math. But I practically skip up the stairs, under the archway and into the classroom, dragging Jasmine along with me. It doesn't hurt when I peek over my shoulder to see Stu, watching me with a half-smile like he's never known anyone quite like me before.

As Jasmine and I start down the back row where we usually sit, Anne hurtles past us. Her head is down, all math business. But then Anne slides a proud look at me. "I knew you'd figure out a way back."

I watch Anne continue by herself to the front of the class-room, where she claims her regular spot, first row, three chairs in. I'm not sure who's more stunned: Jasmine that I'm leading us to the head of the class or Anne that I'm sitting next to her. But they both go with the Patty flow, somehow knowing that I'm on the cusp of an amazing revelation: being part of an all-girl Asian Mafia isn't a bad thing. It just took me a long time to realize that there's something rice-porridge-*môe* comfort-ing in not needing to translate any weird Chinesey things, like Mama going ballistic because I was out with a guy when I should have been home with a book.

"So, do you think the Potluck Mamas are already talking about how I came this close to being a Stanford math camp dropout?" I ask Anne.

Anne looks at me admiringly and gives me a no-biggie shrug. "Who cares what they say? You're going to be a potluck urban legend. Buildering and boys. What's next?"

Now, that's an epitaph I could live with. So I open the note-book Janie gave to me way back before math camp started and write:

## Patty Ho Truth Theorem Four

*Given:* Patty Ho is a potluck urban legend.
No proof necessary. It's a given!

This morning, Professor Drake lectures us about Group Theory, which just so happens to be what my Research Project team is studying. It's actually a fairly straightforward

concept. In math-ese, a Group is a Set with binary opera-
tions that satisfy certain axioms. Sounds scary, but it's not. In
Patty Ho-ese, think of a "Set" of people: me. Anne. Jasmine.
What makes us a Group is that we're bonded together.

Patty + Anne + Jasmine = Asian Mafia Girls = people's assumption that
we're obedient, smart Asian girls who know all the answers in every class.
Patty + Anne + Jasmine = Kung Fu Kick Ass Club = we are strong sepa-
rately, but we are hi-yah! strong together.

Stu passes me a note: "Can you come to the party tonight?"

That's when I remember the math camp shindig tonight. I
wish I could go. I really do, but I shake my head, and catch
his disappointed frown. I promised Mama I'd be back at
Auntie Lu's for dinner. Besides, her permission for me to stay
at math camp definitely did not include going to any parties,
sanctioned by the professors or not.

So I write: "What happens to Stanford men under the full
sun in the Quad? Find out after class."

I watch while Stu's mouth turns up in a sexy smile after
he's read my note. He checks his watch like he's counting
down the milliseconds. And only then do I tune all my brain
cells back into Professor Drake. Almost all of them, anyway.
I catch Stu's eye and wink at him.

As I stand in the middle of the Quad, I decide that when I'm
in Stu's arms, it doesn't matter whether we're kissing under
the moon or sun — full, half or otherwise. It all feels good.

I tilt my head up to study Stu's face. "So you feel different yet?"

"Hmmm," he says, furrowing his eyebrows like he's thinking hard. "Maybe we better try it again."

I lean in for another kiss, not caring that bikes are whizzing past us or that a tour group is approaching on their way to MemChu. That's when I realize what happens to Stanford men and women who kiss in the Quad in broad daylight. They look like a Stanford couple.

"You sure your mom's not lurking somewhere?" he asks against my cheek.

I wish he hadn't said that. Mama's not waiting for me, but Jasmine is. We're supposed to go run the Dish in fifteen minutes. If Janie and Laura could only see me now, they'd be laughing themselves silly, calling me a hypocrite. It's always bugged me how they could cancel plans with me on a whim whenever a boyfriend came on the scene. Our shopping dates? Homework sessions? Poof! Those vanished with this inevitable excuse: "<<Insert current boyfriend's name here>> and I are getting together. We'll go <<insert girlfriend activity here>> another time, OK? You understand, right?"

As much as I want to stay here with Stu, hang out with him all day, I don't want to be one of those girls who blows off her friends. That's not how Kung-Fu Queens treat their Asian Mafia soul sisters.

I pull back from Stu and tell him, "I need to get back to Syn."


**It's been seventeen hours** since I've been wrenched from Synergy, and already my room there doesn't feel like it was ever mine. When I flop on what used to be my bed, under the poster of the toned Chinese climber guy that's back on the wall, it hits me: I don't truly belong here. I tell myself that being a part-time camper is better than being a pulled-out camper, but sometimes optimism is a hard, half-full cup to swallow.

"You should have seen Katie last night," says Jasmine, stripping out of her miniskirt.

"What do you mean?"

"Let's just say, she was hoping to provide a little comfort to Stu, who was majorly bumming." Jasmine pulls on some black workout pants, a jog bra and sneakers for our run. "Not that you have anything to worry about. Did you see his face when he saw you this morning?"

As a matter of fact, I did. And I felt his welcome back kiss in the Quad, thank you very much.

"You sure you can't come tonight?" she asks.

"Positive. I'm homebound every night for the rest of camp."

Jasmine studies me for a moment and then gathers her climbing shoes and backpack. As she does, she says, "Little change in plans then."

A week ago, I would have said, *If you're going to builder, shouldn't you go at night so you don't get caught?* But today I ask, "Can I go with you?"

Jasmine doesn't answer, not with words anyway. She just tosses some stretch pants over to me to wear instead of my running shorts. I take that as a *Get your hapa ass in gear.*

The difference between buildering in the dead of night and buildering in the bright light of day is a couple *thousand* Stanford summer students, professors, staff and visitors, give or take a few. At least, we seem to pass that many on our way to the backside of Encina Hall. Like the scholarly looking woman who zooms down the path, nearly impaling me with her handlebars. She doesn't even notice that I jump off the cement walkway and stumble into the agapanthus, as she races in her own Tour de Trance.

Suddenly, foreboding gives me the shivers all the way down to my scrunched-up toes. I've obviously lost my mind to think that clinging to the side of a building could be "fun." I'm just about to trail after that zombie-biker-woman when Jasmine hands me a pair of soft climbing shoes. Before I can demand where she got shoes my size, she's rummaging in her backpack.

"I can feel you stressing again," she says. "Don't. It's not like we're doing Hoover Tower."

I gulp. HooTow, as it's called, is the 285-foot pinnacle in the Stanford range of buildings, but Jasmine just laughs and tells me that no one's seriously attempted climbing it since the 1970s. As if that makes me feel any better.

"So what are we climbing?" I finally ask.

"The Torture Chamber."

"Jasmine! Don't even give me some BS that it's a perfectly safe route."

"Would you rather do Genocide?" she asks, all innocent bright eyes.

I'm picturing Patricia-cide, with me falling off a thirty-foot-high wall. Two men in short sleeves, one with oversized glasses, meander past, but don't see my panic, they're so engrossed in debating some macroeconomic public policy. I groan softly. But my abject misery doesn't stop Jasmine from kicking off her sneakers and wiggling her feet into the tight climbing shoes. Being out in the open in broad daylight is not the discreet first climb I was picturing, especially not given my firsthand experience with Stanford's security guards. A trespassing citation is just what I don't need, not when I'm already on probation with Mama.

"Isn't there anything else?" I ask, hopefully.

"Sure. If you want to do President's Wall, I'm all for it."

"No," I say quickly. Yeah, why don't I just climb right by the President's window with a little howdy-do shake of my butt? Then everyone at the entire school, including Katie, could watch my hapa ass be permanently thrown out of camp, dorm *and* university. "Torture Chamber sounds great." I try a different tact. "But what if we get caught?"

"Encina isn't the most patrolled place on campus. Besides," Jasmine says with a wicked smile as she puts her hands on the wall, "you can outrun these security guards."

There's a big chasm between imagination and reality. Imagination: I'm a rock star. Reality: I'm going to fall off this rock and see stars. So while Torture Chamber sounds relatively less risky than, say, Hoover Tower, the reality of watching Jasmine traverse the wall, yelling pointers over her shoulder as she thinks of them ("Just find the right edges and you're home free. God, these are tiny!"), isn't exactly reassuring.

When she reaches a low window on the wall, Jasmine climbs gracefully back over to me. As soon as she's a scant four feet from the ground, she lets go and drops nimbly to the dirt.

"Women make great rock climbers with our muscle-to-mass ratio," she says, flexing her toned arms. "So you're going to do great. Now, you're not going to go that far up, just over, OK?"

I nearly laugh hysterically. Yeah, right. Not up, just over.

The sandstone looks miles high and endlessly long. My armpits are tide pools. Antiperspirant slogans play in my head: *Don't let them see you sweat.* Well, it's a little late for that. I wipe my slimy palms off on my black pants, wondering if maybe for the first time in my life, I should have used deodorant, because I can smell my fear.

Jasmine digs around in her backpack and holds out a pouch. "Here, use this chalk. It'll absorb your sweat. Just rub it on your hands," she says, lifting the sack higher to hesitant me. "Usually, we'll avoid using chalk since it leaves a trail, but in this case . . ."

"Usually?" I squeak. There will be no usually in this experience because usually I am sane. I plunge my hands into the sack and bring them out, pancaked in chalk.

"You sure you want to do this?" Jasmine stares first at my doughy hands, and then at me uncertainly. I know that Jasmine's offered me a way to save face, the same way I did with Mama last night, making it sound like Auntie Lu really needed me for the summer.

*Back out,* I tell myself. But instead, I shake the extra chalk off my hands and turn to the Torture Chamber. Just the way Jasmine did, I raise my hands above my head. The sandstone feels warm and rough under my whitened fingertips. I don't say a word, but lift my left foot off the ground. And then I am stuck there, a human crab clinging to vertical wall.

"Look for the edges," says Jasmine.

"I'm looking, I'm looking." There's nothing and I mean nothing but rock that's not meant to be climbed.

Jasmine sighs and taps the block to my right. "Here."

I practically need a magnifying glass to see the one-sixteenth-inch edge she wants me to grip. There is no way that an outcropping of rock the size of a sesame seed is going to support me. No way. But I reach for it and manage to grip the sliver with three fingertips.

"Nice crimp grip! You're a natural," says the chipper coach.

Crimp grip? Try cramp grip. The good thing about struggling to survive is that I don't have time to hyperventilate, not that Jasmine notices. She's back to cheering me on to my sure death.

"OK, looking good. Get up another two feet," she says. "And then you're set for an easy traverse to your right."

I reach one hand higher, and hoist myself up. Muscles I had no idea existed in my forearms tighten as I crimp grip for dear life.

"No wonder your arms look so good," I mutter. When you're hanging onto tiny edges sized for microscopic beings, trust me, either your arms get a good workout or you're splat on the ground. I snicker to myself, only to whimper a moment later. I can't see a single handhold that's within reach. My fingers tense on the rock as my right foot nearly slips off the wall. I'm not proud of it, but I scream. A little. OK, a high-pitched, omigod-I'm-going-to-die kind of scream.

"Reach left," says Jasmine calmly as if she hasn't just masterminded an experiment to prove that, yes, gravity does exist. And I am her five-foot-ten lab rat. "Go back where you just came."

Easy for her to say.

Ms. Sticky-Fingered Gecko could probably hang upside-down with one finger. But I backtrack a foot. And then suddenly, a three-inch protrusion is just above my right hand. I cross my left leg under my right, as I claw for another hold, and a new route reveals itself. It's so weird to always propel forward (go westward, young woman!), only to learn that backtracking is the way to make sense of what's up ahead.

"Beautiful move," Jasmine calls. "See, you're a natural. Which is a good thing."

I can't spare any more than a word, I'm focusing so hard. "Why?"

"Because buildering on this stuff builds up your finger strength. And you'll need that to keep Stu satisfied, hapa mama."

"Jasmine! God!" I can't help but laugh, and lose my tenuous grip. My right arm scrapes hard across the sandstone as I scrabble but don't find a hold. I fall — and land solidly on my two big feet.

"You did it!" Jasmine shouts, throwing her arms around me. "Look!"

Slowly, I look up to see that I've crossed some of the wall. Not all of it, but a lot more than I thought I could do. And only with a scratch or two.

*I survived,* I tell myself and touch the stone once. Just so I'll remember.

"So the climbing gym's open until eleven tonight," says Jasmine.

"Climbing gym?" I wrench away from the wall to stare at her. "You mean, there's an *indoor* climbing gym here?"

"Well, yeah, where do you think I got your shoes?" asks Jasmine, smiling at me lazily. "But isn't being bad more fun?"

She has a point there. So I put my hands back on the sandstone and lift up.

## 27 ∘ Feng Shui

Endorphins and adrenaline pump me up so much after buildering that I could run a marathon even after I reach Auntie Lu's. No one's home when I let myself in, which is a good thing since I probably would have blurted out that I rock — literally. Then, Mama would have asked a million questions, all the while worrying about liability and insurance while insisting that Auntie Lu MapQuest the closest hospital even though I'm perfectly fine.

More than fine, actually.

Just as I'm about to get a drink of water, I hear laughter from the patio. Curious, I look out the window. Mama's back from her seminar after all. But she's not multitasking, checking her voice mail while deadheading flowers, writing lists and logging onto her Blackberry. She's just sitting with Auntie Lu. To be perfectly accurate, she's lounging on the teak chair, looking more relaxed than I remember seeing her. The bistro table is set with a stainless steel, aerodynamic carafe that looks centuries out of place next to the tiny, matte black teapot. In front of each sister are two teacups, one squat and the other tall.

Some of the ladies in the potluck group used to get together a couple of times a year for the Taiwanese tea ceremony, but Mama never had the time. It's a leisurely ceremony, not as formal as its Japanese cousin but with more meaning than an English afternoon tea. The last time Mama performed the tea ceremony with me, I was too sick to go to third grade. She sniffed impatiently when I complained that we didn't have star-shaped peanut-butter-and-strawberry-jelly sandwiches like Janie's tea parties always had.

I could close my eyes and still see Mama's hands preparing the tea. First, she poured hot water into the smaller teacups to warm them. Then, she topped the loose tea leaves in the teapot with water. I sniff the air now and catch the aroma of the rich, dark dragon well tea that Mama splurges on once a year or so. The kind that's harvested in Taiwan, not China.

Out on the patio, Auntie Lu pours the first cups of tea. Immediately, she and Mama dump them out, splashing the tea on the limestone slabs under their feet. That initial cup just washes the leaves. After a minute of steeping, Auntie Lu fills the taller scenting cups, covering them with the tiny teacups. When the tea steeps long enough, both sisters raise the teacup lids and dip their heads like black swans to smell the steam. Only then do they pour the tea from the scenting cups into their drinking cups.

Looking at the two sisters, sipping, sniffing and chatting, no one would believe that only four years separate them. With her graying hair and tired eyes, Mama looks old enough to be Auntie Lu's mother. I can't hear Auntie Lu's toast. Whatever she says makes Mama chuckle so hard she starts to cry.

Maybe what Mama needed was a change in scenery and circumstances, not to reinvent herself, but to reclaim her real self. Just like me.

My heart steams with guilt. As I watch Mama wipe away her tears, I wonder if I'm the one who's aged her. I step quietly away from the window, unable to look at this China Doll Club any longer.

I retreat to Auntie Lu's office, but working on my problem set or my Truth Statement is next to impossible. Even more of a fantasy is any thought of relaxing in the middle of this mess. I can handle the six piles of papers on the floor. And the boxes of photographs crammed into the bookshelves. And even the randomly placed logos, business cards and letterhead that Auntie Lu designs for clients when she isn't making her own art. But the five sticky coffee mugs, two water bottles, eight notepads, eleven pens, stray napkins and a snow drift of sticky pads on her desk? We're talking major skin-crawling anxiety here.

There is no way in feng shui hell that I can sleep another night surrounded with this mind-vomit. I hadn't expected to start space-clearing so soon, but diving into another person's problem is a great cure for guilt.

The whole point of space-clearing is to get rid of clutter so that good luck can ooze into every available nook and cranny. With all the chaos in Auntie Lu's office, luck will need to be clutching a feng shui master in one hand and a sheaf of four-leaf clovers in the other just to find its way in here.

I grab as many cups and half-crumpled napkins as I can carry and nearly drop them all when Auntie Lu speeds around the corner. She stares at my garbage collection and smiles sheepishly. "You're just like your mom."

Now, that's one I don't hear every day.

"She can't stand a messy desk either." Auntie Lu slips into the office and grabs a plate with cookie crumbs. "I sent her out on a walk. She works too hard." Auntie Lu sighs, a small wisp of sadness that curls around us. "So, I take it, you're ready to space-clear my office?"

"It'd be easier to take everything out and start all over."

I interpret Auntie Lu's stricken expression as a no.

Before long, we've got three boxes in front of us. One for things to throw away (a battle because Auntie Lu thinks everything can be recycled into material for her art). One to give away (ditto). And one to keep (bulging at the seams).

"What is this?" I demand, peering inside a moss green bucket. It contains a feng shui master's nightmare: dead flowers. That's the symbol of everything old, decaying and rotten. No dried floral arrangements or withering wreaths are allowed in a feng shui–friendly home. "Mama would freak out if she saw this."

Auntie Lu's face softens. "They're all the flowers Victor sent to me when we were first dating." She places them carefully in the Keep pile.

"Wait a second . . ."

"I thought I'd make paper out of them. Letterpress our names for stationery."

In concept, it's romantic. In reality, it's a concept. The kind you fantasize about, flirt with, but never actually do anything about. "You've been with him for how long?"

"Eight years."

I've always known that living with Victor is why Auntie Lu is only a phone-call-a-year presence in my life. Mama is so hung up on them living together, unmarried, that she claims they're a bad moral influence on me and Abe. As if we've never seen a TV show or read a book or know people who are shacking up without the benefit of a ring.

"Where is he right now?" I ask.

"Africa." Auntie Lu grows animated with pride and hands me a sheaf of photographs off the top of a stack of books. "He's part of a special team of photographers who've been handpicked to put a face on the AIDS crisis there."

"I can see why," I say, riffling through the photos. "His work is amazing."

"He's an amazing man." Auntie Lu looks down at the bucket cradled in her lap and places her hand protectively on its rim. "I'll make paper out of it someday. Really." She glances around the room, overwhelmed since half of the stuff is on the ground and the other half, we haven't even touched. "Maybe we shouldn't space-clear today."

I spot an empty picture frame on the top shelf in her closet and think quickly. "We'll frame one petal, and you can write something mushy about him. But the rest we toss. And then you'll have lots of room for *new* flowers." In answer to her dubious expression, I say, "It's the feng shui way." I stretch up for the picture frame, which is drowning in dust. "When exactly was the last time you space-cleared?"

Auntie Lu grimaces.

"Let me guess. Never." My hand brushes against something hidden behind the frame, but I can't reach it. So I pull a chair over and climb up. Tucked way in the back, pushed against the wall, is an antique Chinese document box. "What's this?" I ask, hopping off the chair.

"I don't know," says Auntie Lu. Clearly, this is a woman who is in dire need of some serious space-clearing. I shudder to think of what all is lurking in the rest of her closets.

Auntie Lu reaches to the side table for a napkin to wipe off the red, chipped lid. "See?" she says, "there's a use for everything."

I groan and toss the now-gray napkin in the Throw Away box. Carefully, Auntie Lu opens the antique box, which smells vaguely like Belly-button Grandmother's office, old with a hint of pepper, cloves and star of anise. Inside the box are photographs that look tea-stained with age. Letters written on light blue airmail paper, all in Chinese. Postcards. An embroidered handkerchief. Tiny seashells. A jade bracelet.

"Look, your mom." Auntie Lu taps a chubby-cheeked girl, grinning mischievously at the camera. I cozy up to Auntie Lu on the sofa bed for a better look. "She used to get in so much trouble all the time." That is hard to imagine, but Auntie Lu sifts through the pictures and tells me stories that don't sound remotely like the Mama I know and live with. How Mama climbed trees instead of doing her homework after school. How she practiced piano by banging out the notes.

And then I stop listening because I see a photograph of Mama, smiling up at a tall white guy with thick brown hair. My father. Ever since I can remember, I always thought Abe looked like a boy version of Mama. In reality, he looks like an Asian-ized version of our dad, with the same unruly hair and the same quirk to his eyebrows like he's forever puzzling over something.

Auntie Lu studies the picture silently over my shoulder.

"Your mother was disowned for being with him. I don't think our parents have talked to her once since she got married to him."

"They're alive?" Mama doesn't talk about my grandparents either. Like she's cut off her entire childhood. And ours. So we live in a bubble with breathing room for only us three.

"Yes." Auntie Lu places the pictures she's holding back in the box. "Your mama told me about your boyfriend. I think she feels bad about how she handled it. It reminded her of our parents. But she was very worried about you. She hadn't talked to you since you started camp, and you know how she worries."

"Well, she basically disowned me in front of everyone."

"Don't say that," says Auntie Lu, sharply.

I glance at her, surprised and hurt by her harsh tone. My eyes drop to the box and the Mama I never knew.

"Being disowned is like not ever being born. All your history is erased. It's a terrible thing, especially since . . ." Her voice trails off.

"Since what?"

Auntie Lu presses her lips together, looking eerily like Mama when she doesn't want a conversation to go any further.

I guess out loud, "Since she did the same thing to you?"

"What? Patty," she says, her voice coated with disappointment, "how can you say that?"

I bite my lower lip, not intending to have spoken my thought aloud . . . even if it is true. Or at least, I think it's true. My gaze falls from Auntie Lu's disapproving eyes down to the photographs I'm holding. Shuffling through the pictures, I stop on one of my parents holding Abe in between them on a rust-colored sofa. No one looks remotely happy in the picture, not the shrieking baby Abe, and certainly not my grim father or my mother, who looks like a kid playing dress-up in her loud purple blouse with enormous shoulder pads.

"Patty," says Auntie Lu gently, "I wish your mama would give Vic a chance, but . . ." Her voice trails off and she eyes the photograph I'm holding. "But I have to cut her some slack. She thinks she's protecting me."

"From what? Being loved? Being happy?" Again, the words spring out of me like they've been tamped down in a tight coil for too long.

"From being hurt."

I release my breath, a *hunh* of my own, and roll my eyes in disbelief.

"She just thinks it would be . . . easier . . . to be with a man from our own culture. Someone who would under-stand how we think. How we do things." Auntie Lu shakes her head. "America, with all our choices and diversity, can be bewildering. And there are some people who don't welcome differences."

I think about Steve Kosanko and how impossible it was for him to accept me, a girl born in America just like him. What was it like to be Mama? To know no one in a foreign land? As I consider this, I rustle through the pictures still in the antique box. And gasp at the same time Auntie Lu does.

Auntie Lu tries to wrestle the picture out of my hand. But I have it gripped tightly like I'm never going to let it go. It's Mama, but not. Her face is raw and puffy. Bruises swell her eyes shut. Her nose is bloated, broken on the bridge. I can't help but picture the tiny bump on Mama's nose, right where her glasses sit.

"You remember?" asks Auntie Lu.

"Remember what?"

Another sigh is my answer. Then, the front door opens. Mama's footsteps go directly into the kitchen, not into the bathroom, not into the office to check on us. But straight to work on dinner.

Auntie Lu, looking every bit as old as Mama, squeezes my hand tight. She murmurs, "You need to talk to your mother."

## 28 ∘ Remember When

You know it's bad when you're wide awake and you have a nightmare. I can't end or escape this new one playing and replaying in my head, now that it's been shaken free. Worse, there's no Brian downstairs for me to talk to. No Jasmine to go buildering with me. And no Stu.

I close my eyes, not that that does any good. My mind doesn't dish up the same old nightmare with a cleaver-wielding father. It's a brand-new, freeze-frame feature: Mama, the victim.

*You remember?*

But what if I don't want to remember? What if I don't want to know why Auntie Lu's home feels so familiar or why she looked so pained like she was the one with the broken face in the picture? What if I don't want to connect all the dots and reconstruct Mama's history via her antique box?

Half the clutter in Auntie Lu's office is gone, leaving plenty of room for bad memories to seep in. Great, I'm choking on remembrances. Or are they scenes that I've choreographed to fill in a history I know nothing about?

There's one way to find out for sure. The clock says it's only nine thirty. So I pad over to the phone and dial home.

"Hello?" It's Abe. In the background, music blares and people are laughing. So Boy Wonder is having himself a party. Suddenly, it's as silent as a monastery during prayer time. I can imagine his frantic motions, signaling everyone to shut up.

"Mama?" he says, sounding tentative.

On another night, I might have let him sweat it out. Honestly? I probably would have done a pretty good imitation of Mama and snapped that I was coming home in two minutes. But not tonight. The last person I want to pretend to be is her. "It's me."

"Patty," he says, all relieved. "Hey, did you get my message that Mama was flying out to check on you?"

"No." I hadn't returned any of Abe's calls either. Or for that matter, any of Janie's or Laura's. I had been so determined to try on a whole new life for myself, that I cast off my past like it was a lifetime of fashion no's. Big mistake, as it turns out.

"Damn." Abe must have made an everything's cool gesture because the music cranks up again, though not as loud. I can hear his friends whooping. "Everything OK?"

"How come you didn't tell me that Dad hit Mama?"

Abe is so quiet on the other end of the line that I wonder if he's gone back to the party and forgotten all about me. But then I realize I barely hear the music or people anymore. I'm guessing he's moved somewhere private, his room maybe. "You were just a baby when it happened."

"But I'm not a baby anymore!" My breath goes all uneven. I feel just as shaky as I did earlier today, facing the back wall of Encina Hall. I didn't back down then. And I'm not backing down now. Using my shoulder to prop the phone to my ear, I swipe my clammy hands on my pajama bottoms. "What happened?"

Again, a long silence.

"Come on, tell me."

"They used to fight all the time, but this time," says Abe, "when I was five, six, they were really going at each other. In the car. Louder than they had ever fought in front of us. We had just eaten pizza to celebrate your birthday."

My birthday. Guilty, I back up to the sofa bed and sit down.

"Mama forgot the credit card at the restaurant. God, even though I covered my ears, I could still hear Dad harping on Mama, calling her stupid because she needed me, a kinder-gartener, to translate for her."

I cringe. How many times have I thought the same exact thing when I heard Mama's broken English as she answered the phone or, worse, talked to my friends?

"She said she *was* stupid . . . for marrying him. And then . . ." Abe's voice goes so quiet, I have to cram the phone to my ear to catch words that I don't want to hear. "Dad started hitting her. I can still see it."

The terrible thing is, I can picture it even though I know there is no possible way I can remember anything from when I was two. Even so, in super slow motion, I see a fist pull back. I hear his hand cracking Mama's nose. How could I not know about this? How could they have kept it from me — Abe, Mama, Auntie Lu?

I pull my knees to my chest like I can hide from the truth.

"Mama got out of the car. She slammed the door and left us with him —"

"What?"

"— and started walking down the sidewalk."

No, I don't want to hear anymore. I don't need to know anymore. My eyes swell with tears and I swipe at them even though there's no Mama here, scolding me to toughen up.

"Dad went crazy, saying that he was going to kill her. You started bawling," says Abe.

"Stop," I say.

But Abe can't stop talking any more than I could stop listening: "And Mama just stood there on the sidewalk and Dad was revving his engine like he was going to run her over. But she came back, got into the car. I always wondered . . ."

Another deep sigh, but I don't know if it's me or Abe or both of us.

"What?" I ask just as Abe starts again, this time in a voice so low, I can barely hear him.

"I always wondered whether she would have kept on walking if you hadn't cried," he whispers.

At first, I can't believe I heard Abe right. Heard his words right. Heard the same wistful envy in his voice that saturates my thoughts whenever I see Mama fawning over him, her favorite. But when his breathing goes heavy like he's been lifting or running stairs, I know I've heard him clearly for the very first time.

I grip the phone so tight to my cheek that my own sniffles echo back in my ear.

"The next morning, as soon as Dad went to work, Mama threw us into the station wagon along with half the house. God, there was a lot of junk in the backseat with us." He barks out a rueful laugh. "Totally random stuff: a rice cooker, spatula, books. She cleaned out the refrigerator, of course."

My snuffly giggle mingles with Abe's. Mama's world was blasting apart, but she remembered to feed us. "So typical Mama," I say.

"Yeah, she kept yelling at me to get you into the car. You didn't listen. So typical you."

A snippet of a memory breaks through thirteen years of forgetting. In my gut, I know this one is true, not manufactured by my imagination or nightmares. I remember Abe trying to reach me through the barricade of kitchen appliances separating us in the backseat, but his arms weren't long enough.

"You tried to buckle me in, right?"

"Yeah," he says, sounding surprised like he had forgotten that detail. "I don't think we wore seatbelts for even a mile all the way to Auntie Lu's."

"Auntie Lu's?"

"We stayed with her for a year before we moved to our own apartment."

Finally, I know why the lotus shoes with the plum blossoms looked so familiar to me. Now I remember trying them on when I didn't think anyone was watching. But even back then, my feet were way too big and I couldn't wedge my heels in. From nowhere, Mama yanked the shoes away from me, snapping that they weren't for my feet.

I hear Abe mutter to someone at his party, "No pot. My mom'll smell it all the way down in California." He clears his throat like he's worried I overheard him, but he's back to being the in-control big brother. "Look, Patty, you know you can call me anytime, right?"

"Right." I know it's true. He's my big brother, the one person Mama says I'll be able to count on if something ever happens to her. But she's always been so tough that I've never been able to picture her hurt. Until now.

"You sure you're OK?"

"Yeah," I answer even though I have serious doubts that I am. All my old assumptions are cracking apart and my heart is covered in their splinters. There never was a loving Daddy. Behind the warrior woman who battled salesclerks and a disobedient daughter was a battered woman. Mama didn't come back just for Abe, her beloved Golden Boy who never does anything wrong. She came back because of me, too, the ho-lee-jing conniving girl who can never do anything right.

Outside the window, the house next door practically gleams with all the lights that are on. Cars pack the driveway, and a woman's laugh spirals up to me. A happy family entertaining happy friends.

Earlier, I told Abe I wasn't a baby anymore, but now, all I want is for Stu to put his arms around me and protect me. Shoot myself up with his kisses so that I'll forget all about Mama, Dad, his fists, me.

I pull on sweats and sneakers, and tiptoe across the floor without worrying about tripping and falling. There's no sound coming from the other rooms. The window easily slides open all the way now that it's no longer blocked by junk.

Leaning out, I stare at the one-story drop to the ground. Just this morning, I wouldn't have dreamed of escaping by window. But after buildering across Encina Hall, shimmying out of a suburban house should be as easy as climbing off a step stool. I slip out the window onto a tiny ledge. Sidestepping carefully, I reach out for the overgrown fig tree.

And just like Mama before me, I sneak out of the house.

∘   ∘   ∘

To put as much distance as I can between Mama and my memories, I start off in a sprint. But it's hard to run when you can't see farther than a couple of feet because your contact lenses are in the bathroom and you're on the verge of crying but can't since you're breathing too hard. Halfway to campus, it dawns on me that I've been running in the dark my whole life. I've always assumed it was my mother who drove my dad away. In reality, she was the one who drove away.

I slow to a jog-limp, holding my cramping side.

My father, he of the fantasy rescues, was the one Mama rescued us from.

As fast as I can, I sprint up the steep hill to where music is blasting out of Synergy. Everybody's partying tonight — Abe, the math groupies, Auntie Lu's next-door neighbors. I'm the lone reveler at my own pity party. I brighten. At least the Synergy party is on a college campus.

College + party = booze.

I am ready to get drunk for the first time in my life, ready to lose total control.

The music literally pounds in the darkened common room, and the thumping bass replaces my own heartbeat. The furniture has been pushed off to the side for a makeshift dance floor. The only people dancing are Jasmine and Anne; a swarm of boys are twitching around them. You honestly couldn't call their jerky motions dancing.

I spot the huge bucket by a couple of kids playing chess. When I paw eagerly into the ice, I pull out nothing but soda. Naturally.

"Patty!" shouts Jasmine over the music and sways over to me. "You escaped."

Now that I'm here, I don't want to talk about Mama and my father. I don't want to hear this techno non-music. I don't want to think about the problem set I blew off. I just want Stu. Being one of the tallest guys in camp, he's hard to miss. But I don't see him in the room, on the dance floor, or with the chess players.

What I do see is the wary look Jasmine exchanges with Anne.

And then, I know. Anyone who confides in one of those women's magazines or daytime talk shows that they had no idea, not the foggiest clue, that their partner was cheating on them is an idiot. I know why Stu's not out here and why Katie of the Big Hair isn't pushing her big boobs against him on the dance floor. I could hide this betrayal in my own Pandora's box, tucking away a new bad memory that I don't want to deal with. I could pretend that nothing is happening, that everything is perfectly fine.

But something is happening. Right now.

I race up the stairs, taking them two at a time.

"Wait!" Jasmine runs right behind me, holding me back on the second-floor landing. Anne brings up the rear. Their nervous glances sandwich me. Jasmine says, "Don't."

But I break free and head up the last flight. My hand is on Stu's door when Jasmine places hers on top of mine and tells me again, "Really, don't."

"Why not? You'd do the same if it was your ex in there with another girl," I say and her hand drops off of mine.

So we are an Asian troika, standing together, when I throw open the door. People say that it's the weird details you remember clearly after the shock wears off. Like that girl on *Oprah* who lost her leg in a shark attack and just remembers a loud POP! Yes, Mama made me watch the show on amazing survivals in case I ever found myself stuck in a crevasse or in the open seas with a shark stalking me.

But Mama and Oprah never prepared me for this. My own personal Torture Chamber, smelling of booze, and my almost-boyfriend in bed with someone else.

What I wish I'd remember is how Stu lifts his head and turns to me, his eyes blurry in drunken surprise. Or how Katie tosses her hair over her shoulder, smirking like she wanted me to find her mashing with him.

But I know what's going to be permanently lodged in my memories is Stu, slurring my name so it sounds like it's spoken with an Asian accent: "Pad-dy?"

When I climbed out of my window tonight, all I wanted was to erase the image of Mama's battered face. What replaces it is no better.

## 29 ∘ Unbinding

On a rare, lucky day, I can shave a fraction of a second off my personal best time running a 10K. But more often than not, I'm a couple seconds over. Now, Mama, I can always count on for accounting accuracy, down to the last cent and down to the last second. It's how she was able to support two kids on her own.

Precisely at five the next morning, her guest room door opens. I sit up straighter on the sofa where I've been waiting since Brian dropped me off around midnight. On the drive home to Auntie Lu's, Brian told me that drunk boys use their little heads to think.

Little heads = big mistakes.

I suppose if I had a little brain, Brian would have made me feel better. But I don't. Which means that my heart feels like a gym floor that Stu's used to practice his dribbling and shooting.

The woman who has judged me every second of my life shuffles down the hall, toting a large black briefcase and pulling a trim suitcase. Her flight doesn't leave for another four hours, but Mama's mantra is that you can never be too early finishing your taxes or getting to the airport.

Even though I don't make a sound or a move, Mama somehow senses that I'm in the room. The sun has barely dawned, yet Mama's eyebrows are already furrowed in permanent concern. "Patty, what you doing?"

I lift her secret box of hurts.

Mama's breath whooshes out in instant recognition. Time may heal all wounds, but it doesn't seem to do much to obliterate certain memories. "*Aiyo*, Patty. Where you find that?"

"Auntie Lu's office when I helped her space-clear." Was that really only twelve hours ago?

I can almost hear every slap and every punch in Mama's answering sigh. I bite my lip, wondering whether I'm doing the right thing. Will bringing up her past accomplish anything? But if there's one thing I've learned from Mrs. Meyers's comments on every one of my papers, it's to "Dig deeper. Give me more." All my life, I've felt like my mouth has been bound shut — don't ask too many questions, don't call attention to yourself, don't complain, just endure. It is generations too late to unbind my great-great-grandmother's feet. But the ties that bind my lips loosen enough for me to whisper the question I have to ask: "Why did you even marry him?"

Mama's lips tighten the way they do when she doesn't think a subject is worth talking about.

"Mama, I saw the picture."

She sits heavily on the chair opposite me, her back to the *tansu* chest and the beautiful shoes that once hid a cruelty I can't imagine. I'm not sure she's going to answer, but she surprises me. "He so nice in Taiwan. We have fun on his motorcycle."

Motorcycle? If I needed more proof that I had no inkling of who Mama really is, I just got it.

"I see his blue eyes. So blue like ocean, sky, freedom. Then we move to America, we have two babies, no money. He still in school. Lots of pressure. Then I know what his blue eyes mean. I lost in air. I drown in water." She sighs and brushes her hair out of her face. "I not trust him with you kids. He already yell lots at Abe. You so cute when baby, Patty. But you grow up. Not so chubby. Not so cute anymore."

Once upon a time a couple of days ago, I would have bristled: *Not so cute anymore? What? Am I ugly now?* But now I'm just startled. She didn't leave Dad just because he was coming after her. She left because she was trying to protect me, too. As I shed my baby fat, I was slimming down and toughening up to become a future punching bag.

Mama's lips purse like she's sipped a batch of my Tonic Soup. "Sometimes people little mean. It take long time to know someone. I not know him when marry him." Mama swats the air sharply in front of her, like she's fanning away a stench. "That so long ago."

At PTA meetings and neighborhood get-togethers, Mama thaws slower than a glacier to new people, and I've always wondered why. Why the only people she considers friends are the ones she's known for at least ten, fifteen years. My eyes go to the luggage next to the front door. Always an escape exit at her fingertips.

A lump the size of her homemade dumplings sticks in my throat. I'm not nodding my head like a bobble head. Not smiling through my hurt like a porcelain-perfect China Doll. It's been my personal policy since seventh grade not to cry in front of Mama, ever. She's so impatient with tears, proof of weakness. I just didn't realize that she had no time to be weak.

"That not important, Patty," she says. "What important now is you —"

I complete her mantra for my life, "Go to good college. Get good job. Find a Good One."

As fast as I wipe away my tears, another one rolls down my cheeks. So I duck my head and study the muted colors of the carpet, hoping Mama doesn't notice that I'm crying.

"I not do good job," Mama says heavily, her words boring into my heart.

I lift my head now and study Mama's downcast face, the gray of her badly permed hair. How could I have mistranslated the lines around her mouth as grooves worn from pure disappointment in me? Some of them might be, but those lines on her forehead and under her eyes are worry. The same worry that compels Mama to hoard articles about dead, dying and damaged girls is the reason why she flew out to check on me. It's not that Mama doesn't trust me so much as she doesn't trust the rest of the world.

"No, Mama, you've been a Good One," I tell her. And I'm surprised at how much I mean it. She may not mother the way Janie's mom does with intimate talks that are more girl-friend than parent, with the easy understanding I've always craved, but Mama's been the Best One she knows how to be. And that is good enough.

"There other boys," Mama says suddenly, patting me on the hand.

My head jerks up to search her eyes again. How did she know? How did she know that the someone I hardly knew had hurt me so much?

"You get Good One later when you go to Stanford. Some-one you friends with long time." Mama looks knowingly at me, her dark eyes that are so much like mine. "You want tea?"

I nod because tea with Mama sounds perfect.

An hour later, Mama is anxious to leave for the airport. She tells Auntie Lu that she can't afford to take any more time off of work. Otherwise, she says, looking more at my aunt than me, she would stay. From the way Auntie Lu nods, I know that they've reached some kind of rapprochement, but one I don't quite understand until I spy Auntie Lu slipping a news-paper article into the *tansu*. Before she does, I read the head-line: "True Love After All These Years." Maybe Mama's decided that whatever Victor's faults and profession — "What pho-tographer do all day? *Hunh!*" — he might be a suitable match for Auntie Lu after all.

My heart squeezes hard when Mama slides into her rental car. I close the car door for her. Auntie Lu is right, I realize. Mama works so hard. Not just because of Abe. But for me, too.

After a quick shower, I head back to Stanford and end up getting all sweaty again after eight minutes because I break into a run. I can't help it. I'm hoping the steady pace of my run will space-clear the thoughts cluttering my head. Instead, it's Palo Alto that disappears quickly under my feet.

So little of what I've known to be the absolute facts in my life are true. I almost feel like calling Abe just to make sure that he's still a pain in my ass. But then I'd just wind up even more confused. Ever since I can remember, I've been jealous of Abe's relationship with Mama, how she dotes on him. How she revels in his every accomplishment. But who else, aside from Abe, did she have when she first immigrated to America? Auntie Lu didn't even move to the states until after I was born.

Soon, I cross El Camino, already congested with morning traffic, and run onto the Stanford campus. When Brian first drove us to the campus, I thought I had a good grip on who I was, but now I'm not so sure anymore. Am I Zebra-woman, trying to outrun a prison of my father's making? Or am I a buildering wannabe, trying to climb to a place I belong?

Or am I just a Stu reject, a girl who's so easily forgotten?

The ghosts of chants and cheers in the Stanford stadium urge me on: *Run faster.*

When I reach Museum Drive, I keep running until I'm on the south side of the Cantor Building. Modern and white, the art museum sticks out on this campus the way I stand out without trying back home. Of all the runs I've done here at Stanford, I've always detoured around the Rodin Sculpture Garden. I mean, who really needs to see *The Gates of Hell* in person when being a mixed-race, mixed-up teenager can be pure hell anyway?

This early in the morning, I am the lone living soul among twenty bronze sculptures. My stomach churns when I reach the couple entwined until eternity in *The Kiss.* So I veer off to Rodin's masterpiece, gravel crunching beneath my sneakers.

Hundreds of roiling figures are climbing, crawling, desperate to stay away from *The Gates of Hell.* Above it all, a miniature version of *The Thinker* sits, staring down as if he's debating whether to suck me into Hell. On the upper right side, I see the Damned Women, trying to wrench themselves off the sculpture.

But I know their fate, and I don't want to be one of them.

I may be a damned exasperating daughter. And a damned lazy student. And a damned jealous sister. But I'm no damned victim.

Even as I lay my hands on the cold bronze, The Gates of Hell slam shut in my head. The clanging scares away all traces of my nightmares.

So I turn on my heel and walk away.

Outside FloMo, I sit in the cool morning air that hasn't yet thawed in the morning sun. I don't have long to wait for breakfast to be over and for the students to stream out of the cafeteria, eager for another day of math.

The first wave doesn't notice me, too busy gossiping about how I got so wasted, Brian had to drive me home. (This does sort of make you wonder how accurate grocery store tabloids can possibly be.) The door opens again, and this time, Jasmine and Anne walk out, their heads together. I know they're talking about me, but not maliciously the way Mrs. Shang would have — Aiyo! *See, this why you date good Taiwanese boy!*

Jasmine spots me first and rushes to my side. "Patty."

"You OK?" asks Anne.

"You bet," I say way too brightly. The way they look at each other, I know they doubt it. But honestly, I feel only a minor fracture in my heart. OK, the minor fracture becomes a major break when Stu staggers out. I tell myself it's because I'm not prepared for Katie, Ms. Afterglow herself, to be chirping up at him.

To be honest, I've seen hungover before, but Stu looks like a walking victim of alcohol poisoning. If this were Boy

Wonder, he'd be hugging the toilet with "stomach flu" for hours. I almost feel sorry for Stu. Almost.

Katie's so busy talking to her audience of one — herself — that she nearly runs into the Asian Mafia before she notices me.

"If I were you, I'd hurry on along to class, girls," she says like a prim and proper lady.

I step out of the shadows. In an amazing transformation seen only once before in the Western world, demure Asian girl inflates into The Dragon Woman. And I bite out those words every teenager who has ever been lectured dreads. And let me assure the world, I have been lectured. So I say, "If I were you . . ."

## The Patty Ho Lecture Series
### Lecture 1: If I Were You

Greetings and welcome to the inaugural season of a new lecture series in an exciting format, melding monologue with martial arts. While this is our lecturer's virgin tour, she has a lifetime of pent-up material. The producers expect this series to be standing room only, appealing mostly to girls who are fed up with being walked on. So please, sit back, relax and enjoy the show.

"If I were you?" I repeat in mock disbelief. "Try, you wish you were me." The Kung Fu Queen stares down the annoying puffball wonder. "But if you were me, you never would have hooked up with someone else's boyfriend. You never would have made snide little comments like you were better than everyone else. The truth is, you're nothing but a big-haired silicone Barbie who needs her Daddy to buy everything for her. Except love. That, you have to steal."

*Hi-yah, White Girl!*

The Kung Fu Queen bows to her fallen opponent. "If I were you, I'd hurry on to class like a good girl."

And then, I turn to Stu, who pales. Smart boy. But if he were really smart, he would have kept his hands to himself.

"Pa . . . Patty," he stutters.

I hold up one hand. "Save it. You're going to tell me you were drunk. That you made a mistake. News flash: you did." I cock my head at him, pun fully intended, thank you very much. "I was gone for one night. You couldn't wait for me for a day?" I shake my head in disgust. "When I walk away from you, take a good look at my hapa ass. Because you'll never have it."

With that, I stalk off for math class. Jasmine follows me on one side, Anne on the other. Against my better judgment, I turn around to take one last look at Stu and Katie, who are both shell-shocked that the quiet, obedient Asian girl has actually stuck up for herself.

Oh, silly me, I forgot the coup de grace. So I tell them, loud and proud, "I deserve better than you."

## 30 ∘ Writer's Block

Auntie Lu and I settle into a comfortable routine for the next few days like I've lived with her my whole life. We do yoga together in the morning. Or, I should say, she does yoga in the morning, and I stay in downward dog. Then she drops me off at Stanford on her way to her art studio. After my TA session in the afternoon, I walk home, help Auntie Lu with dinner and work on my problem sets for a couple of hours while she sketches. A part of me wonders what I'm missing in dorm life. I know I miss hanging out with Jasmine at night. And dropping in on Brian. And weirdly, I miss Anne, my Asian Mafia gal pal who I'll take over any China Doll.

But mostly I'm happy to spend time with Auntie Lu. In a way, I think it's like living with Mama had things been different. While it's strange to be part of a real-world "what if" game — as in, what if Dad hadn't calcified Mama's heart; would she be as open as Auntie Lu? What if Mama didn't bear the burden of being the sole breadwinner; would she surround herself with only beautiful things? — I'm loving getting to know Auntie Lu as a proxy mom.

Besides, dorm life is just a couple years off, and I can wait. There are some perks to being away from the dorm, like not having to see Katie and Stu more than I have to in class. She pretty much stays out of my Hi-Yah! way. So I suppose this means that Malibu Barbie isn't as dumb as I thought she was. And Stu? Let's just say we're both still stewing on what happened, or didn't happen, between us.

Auntie Lu and I are nearly finished space-clearing her home. *Nearly.* You don't get rid of thirteen years' worth of clutter overnight. Or even over a week. But the house is more or less clean enough to start feng shui–ing without any more dire consequences. In hindsight, I should have consulted a feng shui book before I began on Auntie Lu. All the masters warn about space-clearing too quickly; hence, my deluge in not-so-fun discoveries about Mama and Stu.

Feng shui is all about promoting the best flow of energy inside your home. When good luck comes visiting, you want it to linger. So yesterday, we began rearranging furniture and placing it in its most auspicious positions. That meant moving the sofa in the living room to the power-wealth corner. I noticed this morning that Auntie Lu had slid the bamboo plant (a sign of abundance) into the relationship area. I'm guessing that with the mysterious Victor coming home today, she wants to reinforce their love life. Naysayers can snicker all they want about feng shui being a crock of cow dung. But thousands of years of practice in China can't be all wrong. All I can say is that I'm sleeping better now that my feet aren't pointing at the door in the death position. (I made Auntie Lu help me move the sofa bed so I'm facing west.)

While Auntie Lu is doing some last-minute cleaning for Victor's return, I'm out on the patio, supposedly writing my

Truth Statement. What I'm really doing is coloring. There are 5,880 squares on each sheet of graph paper. Half of them are now filled in with black pen. As far as checkerboards go, it's a nice grid. Only I don't think Mrs. Meyers is going to be as impressed as I am.

The problem is, I don't know how to begin. Or where.

"That's a heavy sigh," says Auntie Lu, carrying out a tray with soy crackers and iced tea. She glances down at my grid-locked page. Instead of launching into a lecture, Auntie Lu says "Oh" like she's been trapped inside one of those squares before, too. "Writer's block, huh?"

"I don't know what my teacher wants!"

"Maybe that's the point. Don't think about pleasing her. Write about yourself," says Auntie Lu. She sets down the tray carefully.

"How can I do that without bringing in Mama and the whole Dad mess?"

Auntie Lu's jade bracelets clink together as she pours the iced tea and hands me a glass. "I don't think you can avoid it. Your story starts with them." She takes a long drink of her tea. "But it doesn't have to end with them."

Confusion say: Ah, so, Auntie Lu. You not make no sense.

But then, she does. My hand dips to my belly button. Belly-button Grandmother's predictions, and the reason why I came to Stanford in the first place. How the very suggestion of me ending up with a white guy cemented my destiny at math camp. Only an Asian guy broke my heart.

I start to write. Just like Mama when she's hunkered down with some panicking procrastinator's tax form on April 14, I mumble an absentminded "uh-huh" when Auntie Lu says she's going to space-clear the hallway closet. (That's in the relationship corner of her front hall.) I smile to myself and keep on writing.


The sun is fading when Auntie Lu calls me inside to help with dinner. My head is still fogged in with words and thoughts. I'm hardly aware of the Chinese broccoli I'm washing until Auntie Lu waltzes in, smelling like a field of jasmine. I blink twice. Auntie Lu is wearing a curve-fitting, hoochie-mama red dress. And a full face of makeup.

"Oh, my God! Auntie Lu, you're hot!" I say.

She just bustles around the kitchen doing absolutely nothing: lifting random pots, moving napkins, adjusting the salt-shaker. I bump her with my hip on her second circuit around the kitchen island. "You're nervous about seeing Victor."

Auntie Lu grins the way Janie and Laura, Jasmine and Anne and I do when we talk about the boys we like. She shrugs helplessly.

"Auntie Lu's in lo-ooove." I sound like Abe when he teases me. And now I know why he does it incessantly. It's so much fun to make Auntie Lu blush.

"Yeah," says a deep voice from the hall. "Lucky me."

Victor walks in. For the first time, the real reason why Mama cut off ties to Auntie Lu is transparently clear. Her boyfriend is at least fifteen years older, completely bald and has a large nose that could only be described as beakish. And he's as black as my emergency cell phone that I wish I can use now to call Mama: "Don't be a bigot!"

I'm forgotten the instant Victor drops his leather bag onto the ground and sweeps Auntie Lu into his arms. As discreetly as I can, I try to tiptoe out of the kitchen.

"Hang on," says Victor, stopping my escape. He keeps one arm around Auntie Lu like he can't bear to be apart from her for another millisecond and holds one out to me. "You must be my niece."

"Nice to meet you, Victor."

"Uncle Vic," he corrects and hugs me hard like he's pouring a straight shot of love, cellared for eight years, into me. Auntie Lu's eyes are shining, looking at me like I'm the daughter she's never had.

"Well, ladies, I thank you for going through this effort, but we can just put all this away," says Uncle Vic, already scooping the half-cut vegetables into a Ziploc bag. Auntie Lu looks relieved. She may have an artist's soul, but my aunt could not find her way out of a wok. "We're going out to dinner."

We end up at the same Japanese restaurant where I came with Stu and crowd, the night of my first kiss. Better known as The Night of the Livid Mama.

Tonight, Auntie Lu and Uncle Vic are playing a fast game of verbal Ping-Pong. She keeps asking him about his expedition to Africa, where he's been part of a team photographing AIDS/HIV victims. He keeps trying to change the conversation to hear about Auntie Lu's art, what she's been painting, what the gallery sold and all that. It's funny in a cute way how they'd rather hear about each other than talk about themselves.

I'm basking in their conversation when in through the *noren* walks Stu and what must be his parents. Of all the restaurants in Palo Alto, why does he have to eat here? Stu sees me at the same time, and gets an awkward-awful expression like he wants to talk to me and run away from me all at once. I'm pretty sure I'm wearing the same look since Uncle Vic breaks off in mid-sentence to ask if I'm OK.

I've got to hand it to Stu. He comes straight over to me.

"Hey," he says.

"Hey."

Compared to the conversation at my table about capturing heartbreak and hope on film and canvas, Stu and I sound like complete idiots.

I rally myself enough to make Janie's mother proud by remembering my manners and introducing everyone. Upon hearing Stu's name, Auntie Lu sniffs the way Mama does, her nose wrinkling. Uncle Vic's been home for all of an hour and a half, yet somehow he knows what went down between me and Stu. His brows lower like now he wants to have a "talk" with the young man in some macho, fatherly display of protection.

But I don't need to be protected by anyone but myself. I tell my two would-be bodyguards, "Excuse me for a moment," and ask Stu, "Could you go outside for a second?"

Even though he looks wary, Stu nods. I can feel Auntie Lu and Uncle Vic watching me as I brush through the *noren* with Stu close behind.

The lights in the parking lot flicker on like stage lights. Stu shifts his weight from one foot to another, nervously anticipating the curtains rising up on the second installment of The Patty Ho Lecture Series. He doesn't have to worry.

"So . . . ," he says.

"So," I repeat and look him directly in the eyes, "you hurt me. A lot."

"I know, and I'm really sorry. God, if I could take back that night . . ." His voice drops off and he bows his head. It's a small gesture, but one that wrings my heart out. I've been exactly where he is, standing in front of Mama so ashamed of myself that I can't look her in the eyes.

"So, I got kicked out of camp," he says, softly.

"You did?"

"For drinking. I'm going home tomorrow."

This wasn't what I wanted to happen to Stu. What I do know is that while Mama is wrong about so many things (like writing off Uncle Vic because he's black), she is right about this: I don't know Stu well enough to give him unconditional love. I can't even give him the benefit of the doubt when there's no doubt about what happened with Katie. But what I can give him is forgiveness.

"I'm really sorry," I tell him. And I mean it.

The last binds around my heart slip off, and I fly back into the restaurant, where I know Auntie Lu and Uncle Vic are waiting for me. Though they're holding hands at the table, their eyes are glued on the cloth that conceals me.

When I break through the fabric, their love for me is written in a universal language that anyone could understand.

# 31 ∘ Wordstruck

Once I start writing my Truth Statement, I can't stop the words from rushing out. Every day, right after math camp, I come straight back to Auntie Lu's office to write. Funny how I thought I knew exactly how I felt. And I thought I knew why things happened. And then I write. And as every thought and idea and question drains from my brain to my hand, I realize I knew nothing at all. There are entire worlds within myself to understand and explore.

"You're smiling," says Auntie Lu, finding me in her office just as I set down my pen and flex my fingers. Eagerly, like it's her own Truth Statement that's coming together, she asks, "Well?"

"So far, it's mostly the truth."

I can tell she's dying to read it, but unlike Mama, she doesn't rip it out of my hands without my permission. Before SUMaC, I hoarded my words, doling out only enough to maintain a façade of a happy, clever Patty Ho. The one who's always smiling. The one who is a constant people pleaser. This is my first raw and honest, take-me-or-leave-me coming-out party on paper.

I ask shyly, "Would you read it?"

Auntie Lu grins like I've asked her to go with me to accept a Nobel Prize for literature or something. I hand her the first page. Trust Auntie Lu, she reads it carefully, laughing in all the right places, repeating some of the choicer phrases out loud and even frowning at bits.

"In art, there's a term, terrible beauty. This is it," says Auntie Lu. I brighten because it's exactly the effect I was hoping for. "You have such a way with words." She looks at me thoughtfully before calling, "Hey, Vic!"

"Yup, down here!"

We both look out the window that I climbed through a few nights before, and down to the patio. Auntie Lu is a black-haired Rapunzel with eyes only for Uncle Vic, who is stoking a five-alarm fire for "barbecuing." Since his return, we've had barbecued squab, salmon and baby octopi. ("Men and fire have a primitive connection," Auntie Lu explained to me yesterday.) Not that I'm complaining. Even burnt-to-a-crisp octopi legs are tastier — although somewhat chewier — than most of Auntie Lu's kitchen misadventures.

"Oh, this looks dangerous," Uncle Vic teases, hiding behind his huge oven mitt.

Auntie Lu smiles indulgently at him. "Two beautiful women. Of course, we're dangerous." She blows him a kiss. I would have died of embarrassment just a week ago, but I'm immune to their public displays of affection now. "Who's that friend of yours? The guy who owns a naming company. What's it called?"

"Wordstruck, Jon Sarabhai." Uncle Vic opens the lid to the gas grill and disappears behind the smoke. The only evidence that he's still alive is his holler, "Dinner's done!" I'll say it's done. Crisped chicken assaults my nose. Uncle Vic waves the smoke out of his face. "Now, what are you plotting?"

"Oh, I think Jon just might have the privilege of meeting his future competition," she says, nudging me.

And that's how come on Friday, right after my small group met to discuss the last details of our research project, Uncle Vic drives me to Wordstruck. San Francisco's warehouse district is filled with blocky buildings that were once storage for corporations. More recently, those warehouses headquartered now-defunct Internet companies. Only the factories, auto repair shops and artists' studios remain. We park in front of a flat-topped, squat brick building that looks like it has seen better days. Immediately, I wonder if I'm wasting my time and Uncle Vic's with this informational interview since this company is so obviously struggling.

At least it's got good energy, I think to myself as we approach the bright orange door.

But then we step inside and my misgivings vanish. The lobby walls are mossy green, and opposite the stainless steel reception desk are wild purple armchairs and matching ottomans. A hodgepodge of products are glued right onto a wall: computer games, soft drink bottles, shampoo containers, running shoes, a surfboard, golf clubs, shopping bags, medicine vials. Painted in matte gold over the product mural is the company name: "WORDSTRUCK." I'm so awestruck, I have no words.

A young woman with aggressively short, yellow hair — not blond, but number two pencil yellow — and a nose ring nods at us from the reception desk and pages Jon.

Two seconds later, a human greyhound, all energy and no fat, springs into the lobby. The only thick features on his entire wiry body are his bushy eyebrows.

"Jon!" says Uncle Vic, practically suffocating his friend in a bear hug. I, for one, can testify that these hugs are proof that you can, in fact, be loved to death.

"So you're back in town," Jon gasps once he's released.

"This is my niece, Patty Ho." Vic beams proudly at me. "She's quite the wordie."

"Good, there's not enough of us. Not that I'm complaining." He extends his bony hand out to me, "Jon Sarabhai," and waves to the wall of products. "And all *my* nieces and nephews."

"You named all of these?"

"With my team," Jon says modestly. "So you want to learn about naming products?"

"I didn't know that people actually have jobs to name things."

"Companies, products, features." Jon tells us about some of the more infamous and expensive name flops. Like how Reebok launched a new sneaker called Incubus, which is actually the name of a demon who raped women at night. And how Ford tried to introduce its Pinto car in Brazil, only to discover that Pinto was Brazilian slang for "tiny male genitals." Jon says, "So, the name is everything."

If the name is everything, then that doesn't bode well for me. Until I met Jasmine, I always muttered my name, hoping no one would hear it clearly enough to start with the name-calling.

Uncle Vic says good-bye and tells me he'll pick me up in

a couple of hours. Then Jon guides me through a door marked "The Name Game."

"We neologists create words, and it all starts and ends here in The Lab." Jon steers me down a tangerine hall that opens to a large space, divided into a couple of cubicles. Hundreds of Happy Meal toys dangle from the ceiling. All along the length of one wall are orange, green and purple climbing holds, like an explosion of multicolored acne.

Jon leans against the wall, one hand resting on a climbing hold. "Creating words is half science, half art. You never know what will spark an idea."

To prove his point, Jon sprints over to a cubicle where a young man is playing the air drums to a tune we can't hear. Jon says to me, "I don't want to interrupt his work."

I'm thinking to myself: this is working? But apparently the guy who's cute in an angsty brainy sort of way with thin, wire glasses and longish brown hair is working hard, banging on imaginary drums. Jon pulls a red, squishy ball from a tall, clear jar filled with other brightly colored balls.

"Squeeze," says Jon, handing the ball to me. "Tell me your first thought."

I squeeze, and sure enough, a spark of an idea pops into my head. And it looks like the young man in the cubicle has taken off his earphones to watch us. Jon looks at me expectantly. So I say, "Ummm . . . Boys 'R' Us?"

Ding, ding. Jon bops up and down with excitement. "Right, right, right."

"Nice," says Brainy Boy.

I grin at him, and can hardly believe his double take. It's not a who's-that-weirdo-and-why-is-she-smiling-at-me kind of eye-widening, jaw-dropping look. It's an omigod-she's-smiling-at-ME kind of look. Who knew that moving less than a thousand miles would clear up my ugly duckling syndrome? I'm still no swan, and never will be. I am something different. A firebird, I decide. Judging from Brainy Boy's warm look, he thinks I'm a fiery hot chicky babe, too.

If a name is everything, then I better just say mine. So I extend my hand and get ready for this neologist to have a heyday with my name. "Patty Ho."

Brainy Boy reaches for my hand and stammers, "Tr-Trevor Michaels."

Now, discomfiting a cute guy, that's a Patty Ho first. Oh, and that spark of an idea that Jon mentioned earlier? It's scorching me all the way down to my toes when Trevor grins at me.

*Hosanna,* I think and smile right into his green eyes.

If I had known that clearing out all of Auntie Lu's crap in her office (located in the relationship part of her house, just like my bedroom at home!) would introduce me to a hunkalicious, older guy, I would have finished the job in a single night. Guess who my wordly wise tour guide is? Trevor, the poet. Trevor, the summer intern. Trevor, the soon-to-be-Stanford freshman.

Top Ten Things to Do When I Return to House Ho
  1. Space-clear my bedroom.
  2. Space-clear my bedroom.
  3. Space-clear my bedroom.

4. Space-clear my bedroom.

5. Space-clear my bedroom.

6. Space-clear my bedroom.

7. Space-clear my bedroom.

8. Space-clear my bedroom.

9. Space-clear my bedroom.

10. Space-clear my secret stash of makeup. Maybe it'll clear up my pimples for good!

For the next half-hour, Trevor shows me the rest of the company headquarters and introduces me to some of the employees: a linguist with springy black hair, a lawyer with a pierced nose and a computer guru who looks young enough to be one of the SUMaCers. Trevor and the techie genius, Samantha, talk about the computer program Wordstruck uses to create new words. They sound as excited as Abe gets when he buys a new computer game.

"See, it spits out, like, four hundred word combinations," says the guru, tapping a couple of keys, and the computer starts buzzing away. "See, it identifies morphemes. You know, the smallest units in words that mean something. And the program combines them."

"And then we go through and cross out the ones that won't work as a name, are too hard to pronounce or already exist." Trevor grins proudly like he's the one who's given birth to this program.

Meanwhile, I've coined a new term of my own, no fancy computer necessary. Take the word "babe-u-lous" as in "Isn't that poet absolutely babeulous in his glasses?" Morphemes: babe, you, us. Need I explain further?

I'm smiling to myself, thinking, *Yeah, I could do this for a living* when Trevor stops talking and looks sheepish. "Am I boring you?"

"Oh, no." You keep talking, Brainy Boy. Note to self: tell Jasmine that there's a corollary to her smart girls are sexy theorem. There's nothing sexier than a boy who's not afraid to flex his big brains.

Back at Trevor's cube, he grabs a couple of beanbags and starts juggling them. Suddenly, I'm seeing new meanings for the expression, "Go for the jugular." When he tosses a couple over to me, I give silent thanks to Abe for perpetually throwing things at me: balls, keys, chopsticks . . . even insults.

"Nice reflexes," says Trevor.

I throw the beanbags back at him. "I know."

**Too soon, Jon comes** over to break the news that "Bring Your Hapa to Work Day" is over, and that Uncle Vic is on his way. But first, he leads me to the Brainstorming Chamber, a small room with floor-to-ceiling white boards on two walls. Jon flings himself into one of the chairs and props his feet on the table.

"So," he says, jiggling a foot, "what do you think of this naming gig?"

"I had no idea that this," I gesture to take in Trevor and the whole Brainstorming Chamber, the cubicles, the entire building, "even existed. Or could be so much fun."

"We're the corporate unconscious and subconscious. No one knows we're here, but no one can forget us once we've done our job. Which is about creating an entirely new lexicon," says Jon, swinging his feet onto the floor and now running his fingers along the edge of the table like he's playing scales on a piano. "Meaning, a new vocabulary, our own dictionary for businesses."

"Flexicon," I say.

Jon smiles approvingly. "You got it. Words are flexible and fun. You just have to play with them, put them together to make new words with relevant meanings."

"Twist them like a Rubik's Cube."

"Right. That's exactly right."

Smiling at Jon, I know that I'm exactly right, too. I am a living version of a morpheme, made up of two basic building blocks, one Asian, the other white. So color me perfect. I'm done with trying to be just one color.

On my way to the lobby where Uncle Vic is waiting, I run my hand along the wall, trailing my fingers over the climbing holds, mammoth compared to the slivered edges on sandstone. I figure, bouldering has got to be easier than buildering. So I lift myself onto the wall and I work my way down the hall. Trevor is waiting for me at the other end.

"You look like you've done this before," says Trevor.

"Something like it." I shrug and ask nonchalantly, "You ever try buildering at Stanford?"

"No kidding." Trevor is literally gaping at me like I am the Goddess of All Things.

I am not the Goddess of All Things, but just possibly the Goddess of Some Things, which doesn't include buildering, however sexy that may make me seem to be.

"Climbing really isn't my thing." I tell him the truth and step off the wall, back to the ground where my feet belong. "I run."

"Me, too."

So there we are, Twin Geeks, grinning at each other when Uncle Vic walks in. A couple of weeks ago, I would have been mortified if Mama, or any adult, for that matter, picked me up like I was some kid without her driver's license. Which I am. I mean, who am I kidding? There are worse things than having an uncle who looks seriously happy to be schlepping me around town.

"Well," says Trevor, uncertainly. At loss for words for the first time in hours. "Maybe I'll see you at Stanford."

"I hope so," I say.

And then, three cheers for space-clearing, Trevor hands me a business card with his cell phone number. "Look me up if you ever come down for ProFro weekend or something."

Or something. Nebulous and loose, just the way I want my future.

"I can't leave you alone for three hours," says Uncle Vic to me in the car, his voice completely somber serious. Dread bubbles in my stomach, wondering if maybe, just maybe, Uncle Vic's latent paternal side is rearing its ugly head. I'd never been in the audience for a full-on fatherly lecture, and wasn't so sure I wanted to get one now.

But Uncle Vic starts laughing, a bubbling frothy champagney chortle that makes me want to laugh with him.

"You are just like your Auntie Lu. Just wait till I tell her that your 'educational'" — he makes bunny ear quote signs with his both of his hands — "experience today was nothing but a way for you to meet a guy."

"A hot guy," I correct.

"When you get into Stanford," he says, shaking his head and, thankfully, putting both hands back on the steering wheel, "you're going to have to live with us so that I can keep you under lock and key."

You try, Uncle Vic. Just you try.

# 32 ∘ Math Redux

ere it is, The Big Day. After a month of working with our TAs on The Research Project, slumming in the math library and leafing through the books that the profs brought to us in Synergy, we're ready to present What We've Learned This Summer. So like wannabe professors, we troop group by group to the front of the classroom. It's actually interesting to see how passionate, not to mention proficient, we've all gotten about our subjects. Naturally, Anne kicks butt on her cryptography project, and I even notice Professor Drake jotting down notes like she's given him some new insights.

It could be my imagination, but I think one of the visiting professors sits straighter when Jasmine starts her group's presentation on error-correcting codes. When computers process all the information we demand them to, there's bound to be a mistake at the rate of one in 10 billion. That's where these two guys, Irving Reed and Gustave Solomon, come in. They figured out a speedy quick way to detect problems over mind-boggling amounts of data and correct them before the mistakes happen.

"Imagine error-correcting your choices," says Jasmine, grinning at me.

Yeah, just imagine.

Here's the thing: I can't even count all the moments where error-correcting could have saved me a world of grief . . . like calling Mama right after she phoned. Or giving Anne a chance instead of writing her off. Without SUMaC, I may never have realized that she's actually a loyal romantic trapped in a whiz kid's brain. Come to think of it, was I any different from Steve Kosanko in insta-judging someone based on her looks? Now, that's an epiphany I wasn't prepared for: Steve Kosanko, my evil twin.

Just as I'm about to spiral down that twisted path, it's my group's turn to present. Our team has been decimated with both Stu and Katie kicked out of camp. I'm happy to report that everyone laughs at our jokes about Group Theory and how it relates to the Rubik's Cube. But I get a tiny lump in my throat when David presents Stu's part of the project. My feelings are still a little mixed up about Stu, apparently. As Mama says, though, history is lo-ooong. So who knows if our paths will cross again, maybe even back here at Stanford? (But he'll have to wait in line after Trevor and who knows what other boys I'll meet in my future dorm.)

As I look out into the lecture hall and at the SUMaCers and the teaching assistants and our professors, I wonder if we all aren't missing the point. The most important thing I've learned this summer isn't about how the toy I'm holding is actually a real-world application of a mathematical group.

What I've learned is this: no matter how many combinations of problems and crises life throws you, you can always twist yourself around. Sometimes, you end up in a worse place than you were before. But you can always move somewhere else. I mean, if the twenty-six plastic "cubies" on a Rubik's Cube can have 43,252,003,274,489,856,000 (that's forty-three quintillion!) different positions to choose from, surely an infinitely complex Kung Fu Queen slash Hapa Girl like me has lots of maneuvering room.

And here's the earth-shattering, awesome part. Sometimes, you end up in the best place of all: exactly where you want to be.

Like me, right here, right now.

As Jasmine and I walk into the Quad, I feel a hand holding me back. Somewhere, in the back of my mind, I almost think it's Stu asking for a second chance. (I suppose this really means that I'm not quite over him yet.) But it's Brian. He grins at me and says, "Nice presentation. I knew you had it in you." And then he hands me a piece of graph paper, folded neatly in half. "You dropped this."

"No, I didn't," I say, even as I open the paper. My jaw nearly dislocates because this is what it says:

## SUMaC Truth Theorem One

*Given:* Patty Ho is a hapa.
*Prove:* Patty Ho is like no hapa woman on earth.

| Statement | Reason |
|---|---|
| 1. Patty can do math half-asleep and fall completely asleep during her math. | 1. TA can vouch. |

| | |
|---|---|
| 2. She can talk her way out of more trouble and get into new trouble faster than an entire math camp combined. | 2. Ditto. |
| 3. She can wholly survive a Torture Chamber and House Ho. | 3. Given. |
| Therefore, Patty Ho is an all-brain, all-spunk and all-terrain hapa. | 100% given. |

So what is Patty going to do for the next couple of years, aside from apply to Stanford?

"How did you know about my theorems?" I ask, embarrassed.

"The Big Kahuna surfs all waves — sound and air," says Brian, pretending like he's scanning the horizon for the perfect curl. He drops his arm around my shoulder and knocks me gently under the chin. "I'll see you back here for your freshman year, kiddo."

And when Brian takes his arm away, I notice he's draped his Stanford sweatshirt around my shoulders.

"It's a deal," I say, throwing my arms around my blond-surfer-dude-math-genius of a TA.


On my last night with Auntie Lu, I'm trying to teach her how to make *batsang*, sticky rice wrapped inside two-foot-long bamboo leaves. The rice packages are supposed to be shaped like pyramids. Auntie Lu is hopeless. She keeps forming envelopes.

"Like this." I show her again, twisting the bamboo leaf into a cone before filling it a third of the way with sweet glutinous rice. Auntie Lu tries to copy me, but rice squishes out the top. So I give her mine and fix hers. "See?"

"Uh-huh," she says, but I see she doesn't. That's OK. We all have our strengths.

"You know, I'm going to have a talk with Mama about Uncle Vic," I tell my aunt.

"She's coming around." Auntie Lu doesn't sound too hopeful. "Slowly."

"Then it's time to speed things up. But Auntie Lu?" I bite my lip uncertainly and rush on before I lose my courage. "Why aren't you and Uncle Vic married?"

Auntie Lu's eyebrows lift, blindsided by my question. Without a doubt, Miss Manners would tut-tut at such a rude and forward question, but I really want to know the answer, not just because I'm curious (which I am). Or because it'd take away one more objection that Mama has with Auntie Lu and Uncle Vic (which it would). But mostly because I love how Auntie Lu and Uncle Vic act when they're together.

"Well," she says slowly, "after what happened between my parents and your mother, I suppose I just didn't think any man was worth getting disowned over. Especially if it might not work out anyway."

I look up from my perfectly formed *batsang* and hand it to Auntie Lu to tie with string to keep its shape. "You couldn't create a man who's more perfect for you. Or more in love with you." Rice sticks to my fingers and I turn on the faucet, rinsing the grains off into the sink. "Someone told me that my story starts with my parents. But it doesn't have to end with them."

"A pretty smart someone." Uncle Vic, with his usual impeccable timing, saunters into the kitchen and winks at me before hugging Auntie Lu close. He sniffs the air. "No offense, Lu, but I'm going to miss my niece, and not just for her cooking."

A moment later, Auntie Lu shoots me a sideways glance. "Me, too."

I can tell by the way she's studying Uncle Vic as he picks up her flat, rectangular *batsang* and whistles admiringly at it, that she's rethinking her own Truth Statement. What was true eight years ago may not be true now.

I inhale deeply, and smell the soaking bamboo leaves, stewing meat and boiling peanuts. An unfamiliar wave of homesickness knocks me over. I want to go home to Mama and make sure she's OK. The place I was running from at the beginning of summer is the only place I want to run to now. I just didn't know how to translate Mama's love. It's been there in every *batsang,* every spoonful of Tonic Soup, every lecture, every minute of her overtime at work and every mile she drove from a man she didn't trust with Abe. And me.

## 33 ∘ Homeward Bound

My first day of sophomore year starts with Bowl Fifty-Two of Tonic Soup. After I got home from camp, I decided that since the soup wasn't hurting me, just my taste buds, I could live with it. Especially since it means so much to Mama. Besides, Mama finally told me that the Tonic Soup is supposed to make my eyes glitter. Who am I to snub bright eyes?

But if you want to get all technical, my morning actually started with a phone call from Mr. Harvard himself. From way out in Boston, he tells me, "Look, if Steve Kosanko bugs you, tell the *new* seniors on the baseball team about it. They know what to do."

"Thanks," I say. But I don't need new bodyguards this year. I've got Laura and Janie and Anne. And myself.

Mama drops me off in front of the high school. She's wearing the brand-new sweater I bought for her after we space-cleared her closet and there were only about ten decent shirts and pants, combined, left. I told Mama it was time to start working on her life now that me and Abe are older. So guess who is sitting in the knowledge seat these days? That would be me. Mama insisted that I take Abe's spot so that I'll be open to learning everything before college.

"You be good girl," says Mama.

"I will," I tell her. *Mostly,* I add to myself with a wicked-flavored smile.

Grinning, I rush down the halls toward my locker, passing the seniors who are strutting like they own the halls. Clumps of freshmen dot the hallway and I make an effort to smile re-assuringly at them. High school is hell enough without ghouls like Steve Kosanko and his cronies, including Mark Scranton, lurking up ahead. I don't break my stride, and I don't look down at my feet.

"Yo, Half-breed," Steve says with an ugly leer that's fermented in the summer heat.

My stomach quakes a little, but I lift my eyes to Steve, glaring at him with my best Dragon Woman stare. The pinto-brained wonder must be astonished because he doesn't say another word, and his henchmen part like the Red Sea. So I sail right through them and overhear Mark tell Steve, "OK, cut it out, man." Looks like Mr. Sophomore Class President grew some balls, if not brain cells, over the summer. More power to him.

But halfway down the hall, I turn around slowly, ever so slowly, and pierce Steve Kosanko, racist pig, with another glare. I articulate every word clearly as if English isn't his first language: "My. Name. Is. Patty. Ho."

**"Patty, there you are."** Mrs. Meyers is practically standing guard outside her classroom, waiting for me. She's holding a thick, pink binder with the title *Romance by Numbers*. Anne's novel. So she somehow finished it between all our problem sets and Harry. Even though I know I'm going to hear about it in some potluck group once it gets published — "Anne only fifteen and author! How come you not write book, too?" — I don't feel the slightest poke of jealousy.

The classroom feels different, and it's not just because Mrs. Meyers is teaching the new Basic Oral Communication class to clear up what the school board calls the "annoying vocal patterns of today's youth." I mean, not all teenagers lilt the end of our sentences so that everything we say sounds like a question?

The chalkboard is squeaky clean the way Mrs. Meyers always leaves it. Maybe that's how you need to approach life to make room for fresh new beginnings. Space-clear your home and your past; wipe the slate clean.

I finally figure out what's different. There are a ton of quotes from Toni Morrison, Chinua Achebe, Maya Angelou, Amy Tan, Gabriel García Márquez, Maxine Hong Kingston, Richard Wright, Julia Alvarez.

And above the chalkboard, Mrs. Meyers has hung a new sign: "Honors English Lexicon."

My mouth drops open and she laughs, delighted like a child. "Yes, I plagiarized that idea right out of your Truth Statement." Her eyes twinkle as she hands me a red file folder. "What you wrote was good, very good. You spent more than a summer writing it."

Mrs. Meyers is right. I've waited my whole life to get the truth down onto paper. It's still nothing like the tomes the rest of the class produced a couple of months ago. But it's my truth. Mostly the truth, anyway.

The following is an excerpt from the only A+ ever to be given on an Honors English essay. Which was then edited into a kick-ass college essay. (Can you say, "China Dolls, please Google 'college acceptance.'" Oh, sorry, gals. The founders of Google are from Stanford, too.) Which was then rewritten into a thank-you letter of sorts sent to Belly-button Grandmother, Mrs. Auntie Lu Jackson and the one and only original Dragon Lady who still presides over House Ho.

## Nothing but the Truth (and a few white lies)
### By Patty Ho

The whole truth is, I am Incomplete.

I used to think that was the world's worst fate. Not to be wholly anything. Not to be all white or all Asian, but something in the murky in-between. Not to have a nuclear family with two perfect parents, but a broken family that periodically goes nuclear on each other.

That all changed this summer at math camp, of all places.

I have it from a trusted source that Auguste Rodin considered his opus, The Gates of Hell, to be completed, but not finished.[1] So I figure I'm in good company to be completed (I do have all the requisite DNA strands, after all), yet a woman-in-progress. My incompleteness is something to celebrate. I mean, what do you have to look forward to once you're completely done? Boredom and a six-feet-deep hole is my guess.

My other huge, ambitious work-in-progress is The Official Patty Ho Lexicon to Hapa Life. Incidentally, hapa used to be a derogatory term like gook, chink, nigger or spic, only now it's cool. Kind of like my name. Ho bag is now Hosanna.[2] The truth is, labels are nothing but what we attach to ourselves and to other people, just like labels that are glued onto spaghetti

---

[1] Brian Simmons, SUMaC Camp Counselor cum unofficial Stanford University tour guide.
[2] Created by yours truly upon meeting Trevor Michaels, Stanford freshman cum budding word guru (like me!). Don't worry, Mama, I'm not dating him. Yet.

sauce jars or something. Take off the label and there's a mystery inside (especially if that sauce came out of Auntie Lu's kitchen). I spent a day at a naming lab and here's the amazing thing. People actually get paid big bucks to create new names for regular old things, games to gadgets. Not that I'm going to up and change my name. So don't worry. There'll be no "call me Ishmael" (can you imagine going through life always known as the Moby Dick kid?) or The Girl Formerly Known as Patty Ho. But it's mind-blowing to think that we can create our own selves, our own labels, just as neologists create words.

Fantalicious, isn't it?

My life as I once knew it was all about wishing to be white. On every falling star, with every rub on a Buddha belly, with every touch of my own belly button, I wished I could be more like Janie or Laura or any of the millions of vanilla white girls on earth. I thought life would be easier if I could whitewash myself. So I did. It's funny-sad how you can learn to detest yourself just because a teacher tells you not to speak your mother tongue (literally), or a friend's mother plays Miss Western World Manners and chastises you when you so much as grunt "uh-huh" with a morsel of food in your mouth, or a racist pig hates you for the slant of your eyes.

But then, a pair of amber-colored glasses landed on my face at math camp, and the way I viewed the world completely changed. Completely, as in entirely, as in the whole dim sum cart kind of change. Jasmine, a fearless buildering nymphomaniac,[3] showed me that all I was doing was committing Patricia-cide and killing my inner girl. The only place that landed me was in Sibernation where I isolated myself in my own head.

The truth is, being hapa isn't half-bad, not when I feel mostly good about myself. If I need to whitify myself to fit in, then I'm not hanging out with the right people. That's not to say that being bicultural is any easier than being bipolar, especially when the cultures are polar opposites of each other. I still ping-pong between translating Mama-isms at home, and then practicing

---

[3] Don't worry, Mama, I lived with her, but I didn't adopt her lifestyle. That much.

social graces out in public. If I think it's tough, imagine being one of the first-generationers who had to break the language and culture barrier. That said, in my humble opinion, being fluent in Mama-ese should fulfill all high school foreign language requirements.

Now for some earth-shattering news.

Truth: We are all hapas, in one way or another. Not necessarily half-Asian, but trust me, we are all half-something. Half-good, half-bad. Book smart, street stupid. Math guru, beach bum. Class geek, closet romantic. Student body president, school coward. Boyfriend, jerk. Couldn't we all be in the "check all of the above" category?

Truth: We're all Tourists. Whether it's me feeling like one when I'm at a Chinese restaurant because I don't speak the bo-po-mo-fo language or when I entered SUMaC as the only math-hating camp prisoner. The important thing is to remember that touring is an adventure. Before you know it, you're hanging like one of the natives and having fun — even with math.

Truth: I am still confused about a lot of things. I don't know if I'll track down my father wherever he is or my daughter-disinheriting grandparents in Taiwan. I don't know how to reconcile my mother who was kicked out of her family for being with a white guy, yet has a tough time embracing her virtual brother-in-law for being a black one. All I can say is that Mama still perplexes me, but I know she always puts my best interests first. We just don't always agree on what those best interests are. (Can you say English major and not math?)

So I guess in the end, Belly-button Grandmother was right — my future and past can be read in my belly button. That dimple in my core is what ties me to my mother and to both of my cultures.[4] The black-and-white truth is, my mother's love is tougher than any umbilical cord. So snip at it all you like, but you'll never be able to sever it.

I'm fifteen, and I may be hyphen-thin, but I am not whisper-thin. So Belly-

---

[4] Jasmine wanted our Asian Mafia to pierce our belly buttons on the last day of math camp. But, you know, I don't want to tamper with fate. Who knows what would happen to me if there's a hole in my belly button!?!

button Grandmother, if the Big Accident you predicted was a broken heart, you were right. But I survived. (Thanks!) By all accounts, I'm alive and kicking.

One last thing, there's no white guy in my love life. (Still waiting for that prediction to come true, Belly-button Grandmother. But hey, I'm glad you made it since I got to go to SUMaC!) Then again, my Kung Fu Queen soul sister, Jasmine, has a point. If you want to find the Good One who's right for you, being the United Nations of dating is the only way to go. Hello, world!

And that is the whole yin-yang truth about me, the one and only Patricia Yi-Phen Ho.

# Acknowledgments

The whole truth is, this book would still be a wishful dream without the help and support of many, many people. Above all, my heartfelt thanks go to Steven Malk, agent extraordinaire, and Alvina Ling, gifted editor. All writers should have such a team.

Every woman needs her own Kung Fu Kick-Ass Club, gal pals who are there for the good, the bad and the beautiful. My club began in second grade with original inductees Sayuri Oyama and Julie Yen. Shelli Ching could write the book on True Friendship. My StrataGem soul sisters who give to our community so generously, what would I do without you all — Hilary Benson, Cindy Daugherty, Julie Francavilla, Birgit Gaiger, Julie Kouhia, Martha Mendillo, Lauren Stolzman, Nicole Ueland and Valerie Vasey? Hugs to Sue Lim, Margaret Williams, Kerry Brown, Jen Fukutaki, Stephanie DeVaan, Dana West, and Sophia Everett for urging me to write when I only wanted to chuck my computer.

Special thanks to my beloved writer-buddies, the newest inductees in this Kick-Ass Club, most notably Janet S. Wong, whose belief heartened and humbled me from the very start. Pages of thanks wouldn't even begin to express how much I owe her or my talented writing instructors, Janet Lee Carey, Meg Lippert and Brenda Z. Guiberson. Sarah Hager, Kathy Mikesell Hornbein and Kristin Rowe-Finkbeiner, you were my patient sounding board while I wrote this book.

I like math. I really do. But I will be the first to say that any mathematical errors in this novel are mine alone and not those of the gurus I tapped: Al Lippert, math coach, and Lizzie Hager, MIT whiz kid. Many thanks to Dr. Rick Sommer for creating SUMaC, or Stanford University Math Camp, his bona fide, amazing math program, and for so graciously allowing me to take creative license with it for this book. I encourage kids, particularly girls, to check out SUMaC.

Yes, folks, climbing buildings is as real as math problem sets. I've got two Stanford dudes, Clint C and Bryan P, to thank for helping me pick Patty's routes (not that they necessarily builder themselves — wink, wink). Thanks to Clara Jong, who made me snort over her own fortune-telling experience years ago, and to Carol O'Connell for her accounting savvy.

Most of all, I want to shower my parents, Bob and Ann Chen, with love and gratitude, and remind my incredible kids how grateful I am for every minute with them. And finally, Robert, my story begins and ends with you.